Who Do You Know... Really

JENNIFER GAUL

Fulton Books, Inc.
Meadville, PA

First originally published by Fulton Books 2017

ISBN 978-1-63338-551-1 (Paperback)
ISBN 978-1-63338-552-8 (Digital)

Printed in the United States of America

CHAPTER 1

"THIS IS SHIT." THIS poignant yet succinct phase was what Samantha had become accustomed to hearing every weekend. She got the privilege of hearing her dad's magniloquent tirades in person now. Sam's parents had moved to town several months ago, and it couldn't have been a better time. The love of her life had broken her heart in a million pieces, and on the weekends, she took up refuge at her parents to make the pain less incapacitating.

Sam thought to herself, *He's the love of my life now, but one day soon, I'm sure I'll be referring to him as the emotionally weak imbecile... hopefully.* At this time, he still meant everything to her and just thinking of him, knowing he was gone, made her stomach clench and her eyes fill with tears. She reminisced how Brad abashedly admitted he didn't want to get married after they had already discussed plans of marriage the first year they were together. Thus, after two and a half years of what Sam considered a great relationship, Brad decided marriage wasn't for him yet claimed his feelings for Sam hadn't changed. Sam rolled her eyes and said to herself, *What a total mind fuck.* Needless to say, Sam now hung out with her parents on the weekends, trying to mend the heart Brad had shredded with his inconsistencies.

As Sam pulled up to her parents' house, she wondered what her mom was going to make for lunch. She smiled, knowing her mother will always jump to make her a meal. Sam let herself in the front door

3

and heard dishes clanking in the kitchen. She saw her mother standing in front of the sink washing a plate, and her dad was standing with the refrigerator door propped open, gazing inside.

"Hello, Samantha, have you eaten lunch yet? I can make you a salami, pepperoni, or turkey sandwich," Sam's mother, Brenda, recited as she turned to greet her daughter.

It was like a deli café in her parents' kitchen, and that was one of the reasons Samantha loved to go there. Plus, her mother made the best sandwiches. Brenda was a good cook all around, and there was usually a homemade dessert of some type on the kitchen counter as well.

Sam's mother was the typical plump older woman with a warm, bright smile and sun-darkened skin that gave her a pleasant glow. Her stylish hair was short and worn spiky on the top for a trendy, hip appearance. She had always carried herself with an elegance that only people from that era had the grace and sophistication to pull off, even with the perpetual dishtowel that rested on her shoulder.

"I have not eaten yet, but you're busy, Mom. Don't worry, I can make something for myself."

"Well, make something for your father too."

"Whoa there, Mom, Dad is capable of making his own sandwich. His hands work just as well as mine."

Sam always got a kick out of how her mother catered to her father. Her father, Dan, didn't even retort because he knew Sam was right, but he also knew Brenda would stop whatever she was doing to make him lunch. Sure enough, as soon as Brenda finished drying the dishes she washed, she walked to the fridge and started piling food on the counter to make her husband what he requested. This made Samantha laugh because she understood this was precisely why her parents have been married for over forty years. Compromise. Her mother had learned what kept her husband happy, and in return, Dan also catered to Brenda in his own way.

"You're spoiled," Sam teased her father.

"I do a lot for your mother."

"Like what?"

"I'm the one who gets up in the morning and has to clean your mother's drink glass and whatever snack she decided to eat before bed. Plus I put on the coffee and get her pills ready." They all laughed at this response because Brenda was infamous for snacking at night and Dan loved to give her a hard time about it. But it was all in good fun.

Dan looked remarkable youthful for being a smoker for most of his life. He finally had to give it up a couple of years ago when he had a mild heart attack and now got short of breath easily. The majority of his life, he had always been rail thin and weighed around 135 lbs. until he gave up smoking. He currently had a little belly that he bemoaned about but his family reassured him he looked healthier than he did when his stomach was concave. Plus, he drinks manhattans daily. He rationalized that he gave up his smokes; he was not giving up his drink too. During his working career, he was always bedecked in suits and ties, and since being retired, he invariably wore freshly ironed button-up shirts and slacks. This was his interpretation of casual lounge wear.

Sam idly watched as her mother made her and her father a sandwich, and absently, she pondered her relationship that went sour and contemplated what went wrong. Her thoughts always seemed to flee to the miscalculation of her lost union. She wished she could stop these despondent feelings from overflowing into everything she did, but she felt powerless against the barrage. She tried to dulcify the constant nagging thoughts by acknowledging that Brad was not the man he portrayed himself to be. Yet she was not totally ready to accept that possibility, and it kept her in a stage of suspension from consummately letting go. It always came back to the same unnerving question in Sam's head: *What man says he loves you more than anything but can't be with you because he doesn't love himself?* Brad's aberrant choice to let go of the one person whom he said he loved more than anyone always provoked an irascible response in Sam because it seemed so irrational. She wondered when the day would come where he didn't occupy every thought in her head.

Brad wasn't like most of the guys Samantha usually dated. He was a sweet, deferential man that was a tad on the shy side. He was exceptionally tall with a brawny build. He would talk about his arm span being abnormally long, which helped him as a collegiate athlete, but also laughed at his dolichocephalic shaped head, almost like he was a living caricature of himself. Samantha loved his confidence yet humility and thought he was perfect. When they fell in love, she was positive this was the man she was meant to be with forever, and she truly believed Brad felt the same way about her. She never doubted they would end up together, and that's why it was such a blow when things didn't go the way she expected.

Samantha didn't like to share these feelings with her parents because they'd heard them all too often, and her mother worried about Sam's inability to move past Brad. Sam tended to have a hard time letting go of past boyfriends. She attributed it to her altruistic nature and wanting to fix everyone who had dissonance in their family dynamic. Brad was no exception to Sam's magnanimous ways. Sam was convinced Brad's major malfunction was due to the fact that he hadn't spoken to his mother in over twenty years. She accredited this rejection and abandonment from his mother as an impediment to move toward a lasting loving relationship without fear of dereliction again.

Despite the discord of Brad's family unit, the normal methodical reaction to someone breaking up with another was to be angry at that person and not want to talk to them again. Instead, Sam analyzed the whole situation and felt compelled not to give up on Brad, whom she was convinced just desperately needed someone to love him, even though he had given up on her and their relationship.

Rationally, Samantha knew, if one of her patients experienced the exact same scenario Sam had gone through with Brad, she would counsel them to find someone who deserved their unbridled love. But unfortunately, it was hard for Sam to be objective in her own life.

Samantha Blakeslee was a clinical psychologist and had worked with numerous behavioral disorders throughout her career. She still remembered her first patient during her internship at the behavioral hospital where she was employed. She walked into the room feeling confident and assured, took the seat across the patient, and as soon as she sat, the patient blurted out, "I'm an adult baby." Samantha was stunned and her eyes widened, but she kept her cool and delved into what he thought that statement meant.

"I basically can't control my bowels, so I now piss and shit in a diaper. I'm an adult baby. I also drink from a bottle."

Samantha nodded and thought to herself, *I can't argue with that logic.*

This was way before Maury Povich had guests on his show that used the term *adult babies* to describe themselves and made the disorder more mainstream. Samantha had never encountered an adult baby before or had a text book reference of what that entailed, but just like most neuroses, she knew to explore Piaget's stages of development and discover what happened to inhibit that particular growth.

Samantha had moved past adult babies and had been used on several occasions to help provide expert testimony in criminal trials. She found it fascinating how the seemingly average person could snap and commit a hideous crime no other normal personality would think capable of perpetrating.

Brenda placed the sandwiches in front of Sam and her father and sat down with no plate for herself.

"Mom, where is your sandwich?"

"Oh, I don't want one."

"You've got to eat."

"I just thought I'd eat a piece of leftover cake."

Sam and her dad moaned. "Mom, you've been eyeing that cake the whole time, haven't you?" Sam kidded with her mother.

"Of course she has, you know your mother."

Samantha and her father got a kick out of teasing her about her binging habits, and Brenda laughed along with them as she forked the cake into her mouth.

Samantha was so grateful that she had Brenda and Dan to distract her from obsessing about Brad and feeling sorry for herself. The first five months of the breakup, Sam and Brad were still communicating and expressing that they both were still in love with each other. Brad acknowledged that he needed to work on problems in his past before he could truly be happy. Sam wanted to be there for him but believed their love was strong enough to overcome Brad's past issues. Now, Brad had stopped all communication and had left Samantha feeling even more lost and confused. Spending time with her parents had been the only thing that had temporarily suspended the loneliness of losing the person she wanted to spend her life with. There was nothing better than being surrounded by people who loved you unconditionally and took care of you.

Brenda and Samantha's weekend night ritual had been to watch *Fashion Police* at eleven. They both enjoyed seeing the trendy celebrity attires combined with the churlish commentary of Joan Rivers.

Before their desired show, Sam and her parents decided to watch something they had taped. Brenda maneuvered through all the shows Dan and she had on their DVR.

Sam saw the movie *Black Swan* come up in the list and reported, "*Black Swan* is a good movie… a little on the disturbing, dark side but interesting nevertheless."

Brenda, who was always up for anything, replied, "That's fine with me."

Dan, who was not as easy to please when it came to watching things he hadn't handpicked, replied, "Dark and disturbing—that doesn't sound appealing."

"Dad, give it a try. I can guarantee you'll be intrigued."

"Well, what's it about?"

"A ballerina who is so immersed in her craft to the point of not knowing reality from delusion."

"Hmmm, I don't know. Maybe I'll just head to bed."

"Just give it a shot before you judge, Dad. It's a good movie. Mom, start the movie."

As the melancholy music launched the opening credits, ballerinas filled the screen, gracefully careening their memorized routine.

That was enough for Dan. He abruptly got up and headed to bed, proclaiming, "This is shit."

CHAPTER 2

S AMANTHA'S WEEKLY ROUTINE HADN'T changed since Brad and she broke up, but she missed hearing from him nightly, and life seemed tedious and lonelier. She'd tried getting back in the dating scene but had been left feeling defeated when the chemistry never seemed to be there with the men she met. Logically, she knew she was not going to find someone while her heart still ached for Brad, but realistically, she understood life went on and she had to muster the strength to get through it.

Driving to work, Samantha idly listened to a local radio show that was discussing an article that was written about how hard it is to meet new friends in your thirties. Sam nodded to herself and thought of the plethora of friends she used to have in her twenties. The psychologist in her deduced that ultimately this was the reason people eventually wanted to get married, because people's interests change and staying at home with a loved one sounded more appealing than bar hopping with a bunch of cohorts. She always prided herself as a cool girlfriend because she was generally up for anything—either going out or staying in, she would be perfectly content either way. *Good luck, Brad, finding someone else as easygoing*, she sneered to herself.

She pondered the content of the article the DJ's were discussing and realized she had let a lot of her friendships subside due to spending all her free time with Brad. She felt an overwhelming sense of sadness wash over her. This feeling of deficiency was not attributed to the lack of engagement with her friends, but to the loss of her friendship with Brad. She was definitely at that stage in life where curling up on the couch or doing anything else mundane with a significant other outweighed any bar or party scene being single. Still, she acquiesced that she needed to make more of an effort to contact her girlfriends and play a more active role in integrating herself back into their lives. As she contemplated which girlfriends would embrace her in her time of sorrow, she slammed on the brakes, allowing a Mercedes to squeeze between her and the car in front of her. *Damn Atlanta traffic*, she thought. The one thing that rattled Samantha's nerves more than anything was drivers who didn't use their indicators. How hard is it to turn on your blinker to let other cars know what you're doing? *I'm probably the only person who uses her car horn every day out of frustration*, she thought to herself. Then she reflected on the amount of daily traffic that immersed Atlanta streets and highways and the constant aggravation it caused all drivers and rethought her assessment.

She got to work in one piece, which is a feat in Atlanta, and pulled her black convertible BMW into the office complex where she met with her patients. She smiled as she noticed her co-worker's silver Ford Explorer was in one of the parking spaces, and she wondered if she had a patient in the office.

Sam and Dr. Bridget Ferry shared a counseling office and a long-time friendship. Sam had met Bridget in the social work program at the University of Alabama. They had both decided to get their specialist degree in counseling, and Sam got her doctorate in clinical psychology while Bridget has her PhD in counseling. Their bond started with the same college curriculum, which led to an instant friendship over frat parties and Thursday nights dancing at the Ivory Tusk with the infamous sticky, beer-drenched floors. Hangovers were mended with greasy drive-through deliciousness or decadent Dairy Queen Blizzards. Bridget would accompany Sam back to Destin for their spring breaks, and eventually, they finished their college career, graduating at the same time. Now they shared an office.

Sam knowingly smiled as she passed Bridget's car and glanced inside the back window. There was a baby seat attached to one of the cushions in the back with orange pellets strewn about from the tipped-over box of Goldfish, a stuffed elephant wearing a roll tide T-shirt, a tiny pink sweater draped over the back rest, and papers and crayons scattered along the other seat. Bridget had two small children that took over her vehicle with all their stuff. Every time Sam got in Bridget's car, she had to watch what she might sit on.

Samantha opened the front entrance of her shared office and observed the empty tidy waiting area. The room was painted in a baby-blue hue and was refreshed with an aromatic scent called Hawaiian Breeze to give it the calming sensation of a therapeutic spa. Sam paused to enjoy Vivaldi's *Four Seasons* piping through the speakers, which also aided in the sedative state they hoped to garner for their clients. There was an overstuffed gray-and-blue patterned sofa, matching arm chairs, end tables, and a coffee table with complimentary magazines scattered on the surface. She noticed there was a new *People* magazine lying on top of the *Southern Living* magazine and grabbed it. As she walked toward her office, she glanced in Bridget's doorway to see if she was busy. Bridget was sitting behind her desk with a notepad positioned as a book. She peeked up to see Samantha walking past. Samantha waved at her friend, not wanting to interrupt her work.

"Hey there!" Bridget called out.

Sam stopped and pivoted toward Bridget's office, knowing that was an invitation to come talk to her. She stood outside Bridget's door and looked in. "I didn't want to disturb you if you're busy," Sam told her.

Bridget was sitting behind her ornate mahogany desk. Her natural curly light-brown hair was tied up in a chignon. She was sporting her traditional black oversized cardigan. Sam knew Bridget wore this garb when she had clients coming in. This particular sweater was used to cover up and detract from her rather large breasts. Bridget figured this trick of the trade early on in her career when she caught many of her client's eyes roving to her chest instead of listening to what she was asking them; this included the women clientele.

"That's okay. I'm just going over a patient's notes before he comes in. How was your weekend? How are Brenda and Dan?"

Bridget knew Samantha had been spending a lot of weekends with her parents since she and Brad had broken up. She was not Brad's biggest fan since the breakup. She thought he was a total coward and schmuck to let Samantha go. Bridget classified Brad as a person with avoidant personality disorder—feelings of inadequacy, extreme sensitivity to negative evaluation, and generally had feelings of being unwanted. She had never actually evaluated Brad herself, but when you're a psychologist, you tend to mentally put labels on people's behavior. The labels *narcissist* and *self-centered* had also been heatedly thrown around to describe some of Brad's behavior by Sam's colleague. Bridget, just like most girlfriends, was overprotective of her friend and didn't like to see Sam so crushed and saddened by this man. She too thought they'd get back together when they had initially broken up, especially since Brad was still telling Sam he loved her. His words and lack of action still angered Bridget because she couldn't explain his enigmatic behavior and she knew it was tearing Sam apart. She didn't dare tell Samantha that maybe he was being dishonest about his true feelings because Bridget knew him and didn't think he would be that impassive. But after working with people with so many character flaws, Bridget wouldn't be surprised if Brad was not what he portrayed. She could admit that she liked Brad a lot when Sam and he were dating, but girl code was to trash the ex-boyfriend and find fault in their psyche once they hurt your friend.

"My parents are the best. I'm always highly entertained. We have cocktail hour and we bullshit together. I thoroughly enjoy the time I spend with them and prefer them to most options," Samantha confessed to Bridget.

"I agree, they are pretty great, but you should plan a night out with one of your single friends and find some hot guys to flirt with and buy you drinks." Bridget always nudged Sam to find available men to get her mind elsewhere.

"Ha! Tell me where that happens and I'm there!"

"Girl, please. You've never had a problem with guys paying attention to you."

"Paying attention and paying for drinks are two different things. Men nowadays won't even invest in a drink unless they know there is some kind of return," Samantha said as she winked a couple of times at Bridget to indicate what kind of return she was referring to.

The word most often used to describe Samantha was *sexy*. Samantha humbly attributed that complimentary adjective to her being a confident and strong woman, but it also helped to have her piercing green eyes rimmed with long, dark lashes that were enhanced by her thick, shiny, dark hair and olive skin tone. She also worked out routinely and had always garnished praise for her shapely, athletic legs.

"I am going to make more of an effort to do more things with single people. In fact, I've accepted an invitation to go on a vacation with my friend Megan and a group of people, some I don't even know," Sam relayed to her friend, proud she was taking steps forward away from Brad.

"Is Megan the girl who had the cop boyfriend that you helped with that homicide case?"

"The one and only. I'm probably more thankful than Megan for that relationship. Helping him on that case got my foot in the door for forensic testimony on criminal cases."

"Like we say, there's a reason for everyone you meet. So what are the plans? Where is this vacation?"

"Destin area," Samantha answered.

"Ah, yes, your old stomping grounds. We had so much fun when we used to go down there for spring break."

"Yep, but I don't go back much now that all my family has moved. I hardly recognize it. It has definitely developed since I've lived there. It's so beautiful there that I don't even care who is going on this trip. I know I'll enjoy myself."

Samantha had grown up in Fort Walton Beach back when tourists came to vacation there and Destin had only a couple of restaurants and hotels scattered about. Back then, most people only mentioned Destin as the town you go through on the road that led to Panama City. Now, if Sam told people she was from Fort Walton, they would look at her with a bewildered expression until she said Destin, then everyone knows where she is referring to. She had a lot of great memories from growing up in a beach town and never passed up an opportunity to go back.

"Hopefully there will be a hot, smart, rich, nice man going that you can have wild, passionate sex with to move on from Brad," Bridget teased Sam.

"Ugh, why does everyone want me to have sex with someone else?" Samantha questioned Bridget.

"You know the saying…"

Bridget and Samantha said in unison, "The best way to get over someone is to get under someone."

CHAPTER 3

STANDING BY THE BAR waiting to order a drink, Megan waved across the room as she saw Samantha entering the restaurant. Megan Jones was a statuesque woman with sandy-blond hair and dimples that made her appear to be younger than she was. She was rail-thin and always showed up looking put together with her perfectly coiffed hair and chic attire.

Samantha greeted Megan with a quick hug while Megan asked, "What do you want to drink?"

"It depends, what are your friends like? Do I need something strong?" Samantha jested with Megan.

"Hmmm, the wife of my friend Scott can be a handful, but in a group setting she usually is okay. Otherwise, I'd say do a shot," Megan gibed back.

"Oh, speaking of which, here they come," Megan said as she glanced over Sam's head toward the entrance.

Samantha turned facing the bar and ordered a gin and tonic as Megan walked forward to greet Scott and his wife, Jenni, and Justin and his girlfriend, Kari. Now equipped with a drink in hand, Samantha pivoted back to the group and smiled warmly and extended her greetings, "Hello, I'm Samantha, Megan's friend."

Megan began introductions and Jenni interjected when she was introduced, "That's Jenni with an *i*."

"I'll try to remember that if I ever have to write you a check." Samantha couldn't resist commenting and although it was a little sarcastic, she was just trying to break the ice with a little humor.

Jenni stared at Sam quizzically with her perfectly shaped eyebrows furrowed and a grimace on her face. *I guess she didn't find that humorous*, Sam noted to herself.

Kari was last to be introduced, and as she was shaking Sam's hand, she added, "I also spell my name with an *i* in case you feel like writing me a check." They both laughed, and immediately, Sam felt a sense of camaraderie with Kari.

The rest of the crew arrived and everyone was chatting with each other when Sam whispered to Megan, "I don't think Jenni with an *i* is my biggest fan."

"She's not exactly sunshine and rainbows. I think we all wonder how she scored Scott. She's close with Kari, but even Kari knows she can be a bitch. Don't sweat it. If she instantly liked you, I would have to reevaluate our friendship," Megan sarcastically told Sam.

As the crew mingled with each other, Samantha observed the people she would be traversing with to the beach in a couple weeks. Cassandra Murphy was a petite tan blond who seemed coquettish in her manner. She smiled a lot when talking to the men, and Sam noticed her touching their arms as she laughed, making them appear to be more clever and intriguing than they actually were. There was a lure of sexiness about her that most men would take notice. It was her confidence mixed with her tactile formalities that made men feel like they were special and had a chance with her.

Her friend Misty Forrester was a plain, curvy woman and not as pretty as Cassandra. She had mousy brown hair and a nondescript face that would initially not be rendered memorable, yet she had a simpatico air about her that lent to a natural inclination. She was the type of person that went with the flow even if she wasn't particularly interested in the scene.

The single men, Paul Richards and Chris Fernandez, were both of average height and were handsome in their own way. Their seemingly rehearsed banter with each other was very humorous and witty, making them appear more alluring. Paul's voluminous dark hair looked a lot like an unkempt bush that could use a good pruning. His whole appearance was a little on the slovenly side. His clothes hung on him like he possibly lost weight yet was still sporting the jeans from his former physique. The five o'clock shadow on his face was probably more out of laziness than trying to be macho. Though Sam could tell under the scruff of beard and the unruly hair there was a cute guy peering through.

Chris was half Spanish, half German with dark features. He had small beady eyes, a prominent nose, and high cheekbones. His hair was trimmed short on the sides with a slight tousled look on top.

Scott Beasley, the hunk of the group, had a towering effect standing next to the two comical archetypal men. One could tell he was a natural-born athlete and his physique could emulate with most twenty-somethings. He was classically good looking with thick, dark, wavy hair, a square jaw, full lips, and perfectly straight white teeth. It was hard not to find him attractive. His wife, Jenni, was also comely with a slim figure and highlighted caramel hair. Her big hazel eyes were flecked with gold, radiating a cool haughtiness. Her perfectly painted acrylic nails and surgically enhanced chest exuded a high-maintenance quality while the perpetual scowl on her face didn't convey much warmth.

Kari Stevenson had a cute pixie haircut that went well with her friendly demeanor. She seemed open and genuine with a quick wit. Her boyfriend Justin Ort was a light-skinned strawberry blond who barely spoke and didn't drink alcohol. He was friendly when spoken to but appeared uncomfortable making small talk. They seemed like an odd couple, thought Samantha, but they say opposites attract.

Samantha was engaged in conversation with Cassandra and Misty and asked the conventional questions about what one does for a living and where they resided in Atlanta. It took Paul five minutes to slink his way over to them. He humorously inserted himself in the exchange, intending to get a feel for Sam, the new single girl going on the trip, and charm her with his wiles. Sam thought there was something provocative about the way he would sneer at a comment to challenge you and then act aloof when you gave it back to him. Sam could definitely see many women who would find this kind of raillery intriguing. Unfortunately, her heart wasn't in it. She used to find these types of men stimulating, but after dating a man who had such a decorous approach with no arrogant dialect, she now found these men too arduous.

Kari cut into their circle and singled Samantha out. "It was so good to meet you. I wanted to tell you bye and we'll see you soon." She gave her a friendly hug.

"You're leaving already?"

"Yes, Justin needs to be in bed soon for his early morning run." She smiled at her boyfriend and squeezed his hand.

"It was good to meet you and good to see you all again." Justin said to Sam and the others.

Justin and Paul shook hands, and Cassandra and Misty hugged Kari good-bye.

"They didn't stay long," Sam thought out loud once they left.

"They never do. He's shy and introverted—nice guy, but you don't have to worry about him talking your ear off. Now if you get Kari without him, she's a lot of fun. He adores her, and she likes the attention, so it works for them." Cassandra gave her opinion of Kari and Justin's relationship.

Samantha looked around the bar for Megan and saw her at a high-top table talking to Scott. She scanned the room for Scott's wife. She and Chris were getting drinks at the bar. They grabbed their drinks and joined the rest of the group.

As they walked up, Paul asked Chris, "Did you check out the girl at the bar with the huge"—he hesitated and looked at the women standing before him— "um, brains? She is oozing with intellect."

Samantha scanned the bar area and saw a woman with a spaghetti-strapped tank top barely holding in her cantaloupe-sized breasts.

Cassandra laughed. "We all know where *your* brain is located."

"That's why all the women say it's so big."

Jenni looked disgusted. "Chris isn't as vulgar as you, Paul."

"Really?" Paul wanted to challenge that assertion and prove her wrong. "Chris, did you notice that chick at the bar—yes or no?"

"There is a woman sitting at the bar?" Chris asked innocently.

"Let me rephrase, did you notice the boobs attached to the woman sitting at the bar?"

"When you put it like that, of course I did."

Paul gave Jenni a shit-eating grin. "And there you go."

Cassandra said, "All men are alike. Show me a man who doesn't look at boobs and I'll show you Elton John." She glanced over to the high-top table. "What are Meg and Scott so intensely talking about?"

Jenni rolled her eyes. "They love to discuss work, which is fine with me. Since they used to work together, they know the same people, so I let Megan get an earful when she's around to spare me the dullness. She actually enjoys hearing about it." As Jenni finished her sentence, Megan and Scott walked up to join the group.

Chris made his way around to converse with Samantha and she found him affable and charming. He remembered meeting Sam years ago and asked where she'd been hiding. She explained that she had been dating a guy who lived OTP, which meant outside the perimeter of Atlanta, to clarify where she'd been spending her time for the past three years.

"Why would you date someone OTP?" Paul asked with distaste.

Many people in Atlanta would never entertain the idea of dating someone who didn't actually live inside the perimeter of Atlanta. Samantha found this concept amusing when she first heard of it, but now, after experiencing the distance, she could understand why OTP was considered geographically undesirable.

"I guess you do crazy things for love, huh?" she told him.

"Well, we're glad to have you back." Chris joked, and they all laughed.

At the end of the night, Samantha and Megan walked together to their cars.

"Well, what do you think?" Megan asked Sam.

"I've met some of them before in group settings with you, but overall, I think it will be a fun bunch. I'm just excited to get away for a bit."

"Did Paul or Chris hit on you?"

"Not overtly. Paul has a certain kind of chutzpa when talking to women. It's probably a defense mechanism in case he gets shot down.

I couldn't tell if Chris was hitting on me or if he just takes an interest in what someone says. It's a good quality and also an effective move on his part if he is interested."

"Well, it's usually Paul that is infamous for befriending all of us girls to the point where you're not sure if he's trying to date you or is just a good friend. Inevitably, he goes in for the kiss and succeeds. Nothing ever materializes because of the friendship aspect of the relationship, and I'm not sure he wants more either. His guy friends call him out on it, but he winds up having a lot of friends that are girls."

"Are you one of these girls?"

"Yeah, I've fallen victim of his kissing bandit friendship ploy."

"That's funny. Hopefully I won't get trapped in that insidious web," Samantha said sarcastically.

Megan paused and looked at Samantha with concern. "How are you doing with everything?"

Samantha knew she was referring to Brad. "It's a struggle every day, Meg, I'll be honest. I miss my best friend, and there are times I don't think I'll ever find that happiness again." Like clockwork, Samantha started to tear up.

Megan saw the sadness in her friend's face. "This too shall pass."

Megan had been through heartache with Sam before, yet this time, it seemed more intense and afflictive. She knew that it was consuming agony because Samantha felt true love for Brad.

"That's what I keep telling myself, but the pain still persists." She didn't want to be a total downer so she shook off the sorrow or else she'd become a crying mess. "Oh well, life moves on, and this trip is going to be fun and exciting for all of us."

They exchanged hugs, said their goodnights, and got in their own vehicles. Samantha lingered in her car, staring out of the windshield to an opaque sky, and thought how drastically her life had changed. Tears slid down her cheeks as she reflected on the two couples going on the trip and how she was the single one yet again. She really thought she and Brad would be married, and it was almost surreal to think he was gone. She sighed, wiped her tears, and mused, *Life is very interesting, and you never know what is going to happen.*

CHAPTER 4

THE SMELL OF SAUSAGE cooking always roused Samantha in the mornings when she was staying at her parents' house. Although her parents woke up a lot earlier than Sam, they waited until nine o'clock to motivate her with the aroma of cooking pork to come downstairs for breakfast.

"Ah, look who arose, Sleeping Beauty," Dan said as Samantha walked in the living room with her glasses on and her hair disheveled from sleeping. Far from any beauty Sam had seen, she thought to herself.

"Did I really have a choice? I know you put the sausage on the grill as my alarm clock."

"Works every time."

Dan called to his wife, "Brenda, start the pancakes."

Sam's mother dutifully got up to put the pancake mix on the grill.

Making their way to the breakfast table, Sam observed her dad's sleepwear. "I see you're wearing the pajamas I bought you."

"Yes, I am," Dan said matter-of-factly. "I like them except when I sleep, the covers move my pant legs up to my knees. I kept waking up to pull them down because it was bothering me. I can't figure out how to keep them in place when I sleep. Does that happen to you?"

"Yeah, I guess that does happen, but I've never really pondered the dilemma," Sam said mockingly. "I swear you look for things to bitch about." Sam playfully harassed her father about his diatribe of annoyances.

"Yes, I do." Her father had no qualms in admitting that. Dan continued explaining, "You know I get warm when I sleep but I like a sheet on at least. These pajama pants are light weight but I can feel them creeping up and it's a little irksome. It winds up waking me up."

"Is it really the pants waking you up or Mom's snoring?"

"Well, that's a given. Seriously, I woke up a couple times and had to pull them down."

"Then wear shorts," Samantha said to end the stultifying discussion.

She changed the subject. "Speaking of sleeping, the house we're staying at has five gorgeous bedrooms. It's huge. It's right on the beach and has a pool. We're getting a steal because one of the girl's uncles owns it, and they didn't have it rented out the week we're going. It's close to the Silver Sands Outlets in Destin and the Crab Trap restaurant. I'll have to show you the pictures after breakfast."

"Who all is going? Are there any cute single guys?" Dan inquired.

It's not what a typical dad would ask their daughter, but Sam's father was always concerned about her finding someone now that Brad was gone. Dan really liked Brad and Sam thought he missed him too, but ultimately, he wanted his daughter to be happy and hopefully find someone else he can drink a Manhattan with and shoot the shit.

Sam rolled her eyes and stared at her father. "Really?"

"Yes, really. Why not? You never know."

"There are two single guys going but not really my type. I don't know if anyone would be my type right now… well, unless it was Matthew McConaughey. I'm just planning on relaxing and having a good time. I've previously met most of the people before in social settings, and they all seem like a lot of fun."

Brenda looked at her daughter with concern. "That's good. You deserve to go and have fun. Don't worry about things and relax."

Brenda knew how hard this year had been on her daughter, and although Sam understood she was referring to the Brad situation, her mother didn't like to mention it because she worried it could be a delicate topic. Brenda had liked Brad too when Sam was with him, but since she had seen the pain he had caused her daughter, she wasn't too fond of him. She was the typical mama bear protecting her cub.

"Are you going to see Mia while you're down there?" Brenda asked.

Mia was a good friend of Samantha's whom she'd known since high school. She tried to get down to Fort Walton Beach once a year to visit her.

"Hopefully, either she'll meet us out one night or come to the house and hang out. I even told her she can bring her kids to the private beach behind the house. I doubt she'll do that since her daughter is at that age where she'd be bored, but I'm sure Mia will make the effort to come for some adult time with wine."

"Didn't Mia go through a divorce?"

"Yep," Sam answered, knowing where that question was heading.

"She may be a good person to talk to about things. It sounds like a good time. I'm glad you're getting away, and the beach will be a perfect place to relax and get your mind off things." This was Brenda's way of saying she hoped this was a step for Samantha to move on from Brad.

CHAPTER 5

Six Months Later

THE DULLING SILENCE OF the courtroom when Samantha Blakeslee's name was called inevitably triggered an emotional response that made her conspicuously aware of the magnitude of her testimony. Samantha always felt a wave of anxiousness briefly pass through her body when her name was announced to take the stand as the forensic psychology expert. She was relatively new to the expert testimony role and only had performed these professional obligations a handful of times. She was acutely sensitive of any type of aspersion that she could testify against to ruin a person's life even though she was usually confident in her assessments.

This time, it was unequivocally different than the previous depositions she had been hired to relay in past criminal trials. A flash of convoluted thoughts overwhelmed her as she made her way to the witness stand. It was only six months prior when she had decided to go on vacation to the beach with a bunch of assumingly normal people. The only interest to her, at the time, was to try to find some peace and solace from her labyrinthine thoughts, constantly ruminating on her breakup with Brad. She never, in her wildest dreams, thought that vacation would end up in the court of law testifying to incarcerate another person she had actually met and spent time with.

Samantha walked slowly and deliberately knowing everyone in the courtroom had their eyes on her. Each step, she mused how one could be intimately close to a person and not truly know who they really are. Brad's face instantaneously flashed in her head. She thought, *How can people be genuinely deluded by someone they sleep next to at night, someone they confide their deepest secrets to, someone they think will never hurt them?* This trial solidified to Samantha that she wasn't the only one who felt someone they trusted and loved was a complete stranger to who the real person was underneath the facade.

Friends and loved ones inherently let you down. People are inclined to have flaws. Some people lie, some cheat, some yell and hit, while others manipulate and deceive. But only a few go to the extreme to silence people forever. All these thoughts chased through Samantha's mind as she took a seat behind the partition of the witness stand. She stared straight ahead, awaiting the prosecutor's first question when she locked eyes with the accused. Sam held her gaze, searching for some type of emotion from the blank face but only a stoic expression with an icy glare was returned. It sickened her to see the apathy the accused exhibited for the crime they committed.

She looked through the crowd of observers and saw a bench filled with the acquaintances she lived with that fateful week at the beach. She hadn't seen most of them since leaving Destin after their vacation. She gave them a pursed smile of acknowledgement for the bond that they would forever share. The accused was also one of the guests at the resplendent beach house, which was now marred forever.

Also in the audience was her high school friend Mia and her friend who practiced law in Atlanta, Trey. Trey drove down that morning to give Sam support, and since he was very familiar with a courtroom, he figured he could be of any assistance if needed. Plus, he had a condo in Destin where they would stay a couple of days after the trial to relax and put the last six months behind Sam.

Samantha came down a day earlier to spend time with Mia, and during dinner and drinks, they discussed the case. After having several glasses of wine, Mia swore that she knew all along who the guilty member of the group was. Sam laughed at her averment. Mia had spent some time with the household guest six months prior when they were down, but Sam knew she didn't know any of them well enough to assess this kind of judgment.

"Mia, you're so full of shit. You couldn't even name half the people staying in that house at that time," Sam lightheartedly ridiculed Mia.

"Oh, I knew," she slurred back at Samantha.

"Really? What did you know? If I remember correctly, you bolted out of there and never told me you suspected anyone."

"That's only because I knew you'd figure it out and I didn't want to step on your toes."

"Ah, is that right? Well, I'm glad I now know I can always call you if I ever need any assistance with forensic psychology." Sam went along with Mia's befuddled declaration.

"Well, of course you can. Check out that guy at the bar. He's delicious." Sam was grateful Mia was on to the next subject.

Samantha walked the prosecutor, jury, and audience through her computations of what had occurred the night that was in question. She did notice the head of the accused dropped when she relayed the brutality of the action taken toward the victim. This gave Samantha a tad bit of peace, knowing there was some type of culpability and maybe even remorse. The accused was pleading "not guilty," knowing there was slim to no evidence linking them to the crime. The whole house was a witness to this person basically admitting to the crime, but it was one word against another, and without hard, palpable evidence, some guilty people have walked free.

It was a long trial, and the jury took a day to deliberate and come to a verdict. Samantha and the crew from the beach house had all gone to dinner the day the lawyers finished with their closing arguments. The beach house crew spoke in depth over dinner of the trial. Sam knew everyone's opinion on the accused and the desired penalty.

They all convened at the courtroom a day later to anticipate the final decision from the jury. After the jury foreman read the verdict, Sam knew everyone was glad to be able to put this behind them. She wondered what the crew thought about the minimal sentence. They did have an interesting conversation over dinner about people that snapped and committed hideous crimes. She almost felt there was a tinge of sympathy for the accused from some of the beach house crew. They all wanted there to be justice for what occurred, but Sam wondered how many of them questioned their own psyche if put in a situation that could possibly make them snap.

CHAPTER 6

CRUISING DOWN THE INTERSTATE in a convertible was the only way to travel when heading to the beach. That's why Samantha got stuck driving to Destin. She told Megan that she'd drive down there with her convertible as long as Megan would be the one to drive her car back to Atlanta. Samantha would much rather be the passenger in a vehicle than endure the numerous, erratic, inattentive drivers on the road. Driving in Atlanta had made her über sensitive to the dangers and maniacs on the road.

Plus driving to any vacation locale was a much easier ride than the drive back. The excitement of getting there and being off from work made the trip fly. Usually, the ride home, everyone was tired and a little weary of the people they had been with for the past week. That was why she made the deal to have Megan drive them back home. Sam figured she could zone out then and take a nap, but now Samantha and Megan had a lot to talk about. Sam was inquisitive about the people they would be spending the next several days with.

"Before I start drilling you on the gossip of the others coming on this trip, what's been going on with you… any new men in your life?"

Megan was habitually on some dating website and usually had a couple guys she was texting, but she had a hard time materializing a relationship. She took rejection hard and, Samantha was always trying to tell her not to take a one date wonder too personally. Sam reasoned that after one date, they didn't really know her and she didn't truly know what was going on in their lives to detract them.

Megan hesitated to answer, so Samantha glanced at her friend to see if she heard her. Megan then replied, "Nah, nothing to really talk about. You know, it's the same old BS dating scene. The hot ones are gay, and the good ones are taken."

Samantha felt like Megan wasn't telling her something, but she understood how the dating scene went, and usually it was hit or miss, with a whole hell of a lot more misses than hits.

"Girl, that's what scares me the most now that I'm single again. I really thought Brad was the one and I wouldn't be back on the market looking for Mr. Right again. It's so depressing."

"You're preaching to the choir! I hate all men... well, until I meet the right one, you know?" They both laughed and agreed the woes of dating were imminent.

"So what's the scoop on any of these people we're going to be with at the beach?"

"Let's see. Paul can be witty and funny if you like his kind of humor. Meaning, he can come off as a total asshole, but it's a dry wit and I find it amusing. For example, when Paul's ex-girlfriend's child yelled at him, 'You are not my dad!' Paul calmly responded, 'Yes, you're right. I have hair and I'm better-looking.' That's his type of humor. It was totally lost on an eight-year-old, but I thought it was hysterical. People with kids are less likely to find that funny, but when he told the context of the situation and the way he said it, I got a kick out of it. His best friend Chris is also funny and witty but not mean in his delivery. They both are not the best-looking guys you've ever seen, but they have no problem getting women."

"You mean like every guy in Atlanta?"

"Ain't that the truth."

Samantha and Megan always ruminated on how it seemed even the most obscure man in Atlanta could find a girlfriend any night of the week yet there were tons of single, attractive, successful women in Atlanta that couldn't find a decent man to date if their life depended on it.

They both grunted their dismay over their perceived plight.

"Anyway, Cassandra is a huge flirt and would flirt with the lamppost if there were no men around. She's a lot of fun. I feel like Jenni feels some rivalry toward Cassandra because Cassandra is pretty and gets a lot of attention from men. Rumor has it that when Jenni was single, Cass and she vied for many of the same men. I guess that rivalry is still somewhat embedded in Jenni, although she's married. Who knows?"

"I hope I'd become the biggest cheerleader for a single friend if I finally found my husband," Sam commented.

"Yeah, one would think. Jenni is not one of those supportive women that has your back and cheers for someone's happiness. She basically looks out for number one and will step on whomever to get what she wants."

"Sign me up to be her best friend," Sam said sarcastically. "What about the rest?"

"I don't know Misty well, but she is always super sweet. Scott, as you know, is gorgeous and perfect. I originally met him because we worked together. Personally, I don't think he's that happy being married. Jenni can be a real drag and always seems to be caught up in some drama."

"Well, if she's how you describe her, then he should have known. Looks only go so far. Do the others get annoyed with her behavior?"

"Paul most definitely does. Jenni and Paul bicker a lot because Paul would insult her and she takes it way too personally. This just eggs Paul on to do it more. Scott and Paul are friends, so Scott doesn't get involved when he picks on his wife and that also gets Jenni's goat. Jenni finds Paul offensive and crude. She acts like she's too pristine for Paul's obscene jokes.

"Kari is funny and personable yet is dating a stick in the mud. Justin hardly speaks and doesn't drink so he always seems like the odd man out. Scott says he avoids doing things with just the four of them because Justin doesn't have a lot to say. He tried out for the Navy Seals but was supposedly turned down for some character flaw. I'm assuming it was because he's too sensitive or something like that yet he made the Green Berets so who knows. It's such an oxymoron because he is seriously so shy and quiet that you'd never think he could be a badass in the military."

"Interesting apercu. I guess now I know why Jenni doesn't care for me," Samantha stated.

"Because you use words like *apercu*?"

"Funny."

"Why?"

"Um, hello, if she's jealous of Cassandra because she's pretty…" Sam pointed her finger and gestured up and down her body. "Have you seen this?" They both burst out laughing. Even though Samantha was very attractive, she loved to mock the whole context of beauty.

Five hours later, they pulled into the driveway of a huge, majestic beach house. As their eyes marveled at the full extent of the mansion, they turned toward each other and were in agreement of the impressiveness of their abode for the week and became giddy with excitement.

Paul's Yukon was parked in the circular drive. He drove Misty, Cassandra, and Chris. The two couples were traveling together but had not yet arrived. Samantha and Megan hurriedly gathered their bags and headed up the stoned entryway to the grand, windowed, double front doors. They were excited to get their vacation started.

The door wasn't locked, so they walked in, calling out, "Hello, we're here."

They waited for a response but were greeted with silence. They shrugged and continued through the foyer to the open-layout kitchen and living room. The rear of the house was lined with floor-to-ceiling glass walls overlooking the beach and the blue-green crystal gulf water. Sam immediately felt at home seeing the sun glisten off the gulf. The impressive sight induced a tranquility felt by both girls. Abstractedly, Sam let out a carefree sigh. The beach always conjured many nostalgic memories for Samantha. The water drew the girls closer to the windows for a better view. Megan spotted the four other guests exploring the pool below.

"It looks like they just got here too. Let's put our stuff away and grab a cocktail and see if they want to go somewhere for lunch."

Samantha and Megan picked an unoccupied bedroom, and Megan immediately had to put her folded clothes in the empty dresser and placed her hanging clothes in the closet.

"Are you always this orderly when you pack?" Sam asked, admiring the meticulous way Megan's suitcase was packed and unpacked so swiftly.

"I'm a little OCD about gathering my things and keeping order. I hardly ever forget anything, and I know where everything is."

Sam shrugged as she opened her suitcase and hung up one dress and left the other clothes in her bag, not wanting to bother putting them away at this time. "I figure if I forget something, like my toothbrush, I can either buy it wherever I'm at or if I forget a shirt I wanted to pack, then I'm shit out of luck." Megan stared at her like she was speaking a foreign language.

They headed back downstairs to greet the others and make a drink. They saw Paul and Chris were in the kitchen making cocktails and Misty and Cassandra were sitting on the bar stools, waiting to be served.

"Hey, guys. We didn't know y'all were here," Cassandra said as she spotted Samantha and Megan walking down the stairs.

"Yep, we just got here. We picked a room and wanted to put our things up. What are you making, Chris?" Megan asked.

"Anything you want. We brought almost any type of liquor you can imagine."

"We brought some flavor-infused vodka and beer. I think I'll just stick with beer right now," Sam told Chris. Paul immediately reached for the fridge and materialized a Blue Moon for Sam. He sliced an orange and put it on the rim of a beer glass.

"Wow, apparently we don't need to leave the house with this kind of service."

Paul winked at her and gave her two gun gestures with his hands.

"I want a fun drink. Chris, whatever you're making, I'll have one too. We're hungry also. Do you guys want to go to a beach bar and get lunch? Should we wait for Scott and the rest to get here… what are you guys thinking?" Megan asked the crew.

"They're running late. Scott texted Paul," Misty answered.

"You know it had to be Jenni that couldn't get out the door in time," Cass chimed in.

"I'm glad I drove and didn't get stuck riding with Jenni. I can hear her now—'The air is too cold, now it's too hot, this is taking too long, are we there yet, I have to go pee, I'm hungry.'" Paul imitated Jenni's voice in a high-pitched whine. "She is the most high-maintenance girl I've ever met. I give Scott a lot of props for being able to put up with her ass. I would have used her for sex and gotten rid of her a long time ago."

Cass rolled her eyes. "You're such a pig."

"Oink, oink," Paul mimicked.

"So in other words, we don't have to wait around for them because it might be longer than an hour?" Megan tried to get the conversation back on track.

Cassandra fished through her purse and retrieved her cell phone. "Let me call Kari and see where they're at, and I'll tell them we're going to go eat and see if they can meet us."

While Cassandra called Kari, the others discussed what they wanted to do that night.

"I think we should make a grocery list for dinner and cookout tonight and drink by the pool," Chris suggested.

"I would be totally down with that also," Sam said as Misty and Megan nodded in agreement.

With everyone on the same page, Paul requested an activity for the night. "All the women have to skinny-dip and do naked synchronized swimming and the men will judge who the winner will be. Cass, we've all seen you naked, so you don't have to participate— we've all been there, done that." Paul poked at Cassandra.

Paul loved to take jabs at Cassandra's promiscuity only because she always had male admirers around her and she was a chronic flirt. Plus, because Paul was infamous for kissing most of his female friends, he liked to insinuate that there may have been more that went on between him and Cassandra. This was his way of letting people know Cassandra was probably one of his girlfriends that had fallen prey to his charms.

"Yeah, right. You wish. You're an asshole." Cassandra punched Paul in his arm as he walked by.

"Better than being a Cass-hole," he gibed back at her.

Paul tossed Cassandra a blue tablet. "Here, write a grocery list of what we need tonight for dinner."

Sam noticed Misty casually staring and smiling at Paul and she wondered if she had a little crush on him.

CHAPTER 7

Pulling the Yukon in the circular driveway, they all noticed Scott's car was now parked next to Sam's convertible.

"I hope they like what we got for dinner tonight. I forgot to ask them where they were stopping to eat on their way here," Cassandra said to the group in the car.

"I'm sure it will be fine," Misty offered up.

They gathered up the groceries and headed in the house.

"Ah, they're at the pool. Let's get on our bathing suits and join them," Megan said as she ascended the stairs to her and Sam's room.

Misty stayed behind in the kitchen to help Paul put the groceries away.

Sam said to Megan as they climbed the stairs, "I think Misty has a crush on Paul."

"Hmm, you think? Paul will probably hook up with her, but I don't see him dating her," Megan said nonchalantly.

"Really, why? She's so sweet."

"That's exactly the reason why. He needs someone that can give him shit back. She'd bore him."

Downstairs, Chris walked out to the porch and yelled down to the others at the pool. "Does anyone need a cocktail?"

Scott yelled back. "We have a cooler of beer down here."

Jenni called back to Chris, "You can make me a margarita… with salt."

Jenni and Chris had gone out a couple times in the distant past before she met her husband, Scott. Jenni knew that Chris still had a crush on her, and she thrived on it because Chris would do almost anything she asked. She maintained a friendly, flirtatious relationship with him mainly for this purpose.

Chris walked back in the house and looked at Paul and Misty and said, "She just assumes I'll make her a margarita although she didn't even ask what cocktails I was making or ask if I *would* make her a margarita."

"Who?" Misty inquired.

"Really, you have to ask? Let me guess… Jen-needy?" Paul asked Chris.

"Yes, Jen-needy."

Misty giggled at Chris and Paul's alias for Jenni. She didn't know that was their nickname for her, but she had to admit it was fitting.

"Dude, make her a vodka and sprite and tell her that's what you were making and either she can drink it or make her own drink," Paul told Chris.

Chris nodded, "Yeah, her demanding ass needs to make her husband get her what she wants." He said this while he was searching for the margarita mix.

At the pool, Samantha took the empty seat next to Jenni. At first, Jenni was very complimentary to Sam. She praised her choice of swimsuit and said she admired her figure. Then she started peppering Sam with questions about herself.

"So what do you do for a living, Sam?"

"I'm a psychologist."

"Really? That's interesting. So you basically analyze everyone you meet."

"Yeah, that's about right." Sam looked at Jenni to see if she smiled. Jenni just stared back at her with no hint of a grin.

"I'm kidding." Sam playfully slapped Jenni's arm. "I analyze people the same as you would when you meet someone new. I get that comment a lot, but I really don't think my assessment of people, in a social context, is any different than the normal analysis by any other person. I don't put too much thought in analyzing people unless I'm getting paid for it," Samantha explained to Jenni with a laugh.

Jenni didn't laugh and, instead, turned her head toward her husband, where he was gleefully laughing, standing in the pool, talking to Megan and Cassandra. Her eyes narrowed briefly, but then she turned back to Samantha and continued with her questioning. "So are you seeing anyone?"

"I just got out of a long relationship. I'm pretty much broken-hearted right now. You're lucky to have found your husband. It seems like an impossible task in Atlanta. How did you guys meet?"

"Humph, married life isn't all it's cracked up to be." Then Jenni seemed to catch herself and said, "Well, don't get me wrong—it's great, and I have a wonderful husband, but I'm one of the lucky ones. But there are a lot of unhappy married people. We met at a party and it was love at first sight. We've been going strong ever since."

It was obvious Jenni was projecting her own feelings about marriage, but she didn't feel comfortable enough to admit it to Samantha. Sam could tell Jenni was the type of person who would put on a façade that everything was perfect in her life although it was crumbling around her.

Hmm, maybe I do analyze people more than the average person. Nah, anyone would make that analysis... right? Sam thought, second-guessing herself.

Kari walked over to Sam and Jenni and sat on the bottom part of Jenni's lounge chair. Kari had been keeping her boyfriend, Justin, company. He was stuck sitting alone under a big umbrella since his skin type was prone to burn.

"How is Justin faring in this sun?" Samantha asked to take an interest.

"He isn't a big sun person, but he enjoys relaxing. As long as there is shade for him, he'll be fine."

Jenni, who didn't find talk of Justin remotely interesting, changed the subject. "Go jump on Scott and get his hair wet. You know he takes forever to style his hair. It will be funny," Jenni incited Kari.

Kari, who was always up for excitement, obliged Jenni's request.

This was Jenni's way to break up the conversation between Megan, Cass, and Scott. Jenni didn't like Cassandra to spend too much time with her husband with her come-hither mannerisms, especially in her bathing suit.

"Justin is such a bore that I want Kari to have some fun," Jenni explained to Sam as she watched Kari wander over to the edge of the pool.

"He is shy or introverted and may not have a lot to say, but I guess Kari finds something enticing about him," Sam said to be nice.

"I don't know what. Look at him now."

They both turned to look at Justin just after Kari vaulted off the side of the pool onto Scott's back. Kari was screaming with ferment as Scott was trying to dunk her before she could get him under. Yet there was no expression on Justin's face as he stared at Kari intently.

"He's so weird. He constantly watches Kari and will just ogle her. It's really creepy."

"Or he really loves her and it's kind of sweet," Samantha offered.

Jenni rolled her eyes and turned away from Samantha as she said, "Whatever."

CHAPTER 8

THE FIRST NIGHT AT the beach house the crew had decided to stay in and cook dinner together and unwind. The men had been drinking all day, except for Justin, and were equipped to keep going. Most of the women had taken a break from drinking and either took a nap before dinner or gossiped at the pool.

Samantha stood on the deck with Paul and Chris as they manned the burgers on the grill. They were asking Samantha about her relationship with Brad and what happened.

Sam explained that she always thought she and Brad were on the same page about marriage and even talked about where they'd do it. But when it came to the next step, Brad did the inconceivable and decided to walk away.

Paul's advice was, "Fuck him. He did you a favor. Better you know now."

This was the sentiment she got from most men about her failed relationship, and she wished it was that easy to blow it off and move on.

Chris offered up his encouragement. "I am available, you know. Not to brag, but I am hung like a tuna can."

"Why would I want a tuna can?" Samantha asked with a look of bewilderment on her face.

"Think about what a tuna can looks like…" Chris cajoled Sam. "It's short and fat."

"Exactly," Chris said as he moved his eyebrows up and down.

Samantha laughed out loud.

"If the tuna can is not your thing I've been labeled a golf pencil," Paul interjected.

Their deadpan delivery made this amusing, and it was obviously a routine shtick they've done before.

"Well, guys, I'll definitely keep both those visuals in mind in case I feel in the mood for fish or to write something down." She giggled thinking about it. "Don't you want to keep your pencil sharpened for someone else in this house?" Sam asked Paul.

"Who are you referring?"

"Oh, come on. You must know that Misty hangs on your every word. She's a sweet girl. You should go for it."

Paul flipped the burgers and said, "What can I say? All women want my meat."

He then placed a burger on a plate and handed it to Sam. "Here, you can have my meat too."

Sam took the plate, "There is something perversely charming about you."

Paul grinned and looked at his friend. "Chris, I think she prefers the golf pencil."

Later that night, everyone was having a fun time drinking and playing games together. Justin and Kari had gone to bed earlier since Justin didn't drink and the games inevitably turned into drinking games. Jenni started out in a good mood and was blending in with the crowd, but before long, she started being condescending with her pejorative remarks.

Paul had been teasing her by calling her "Jen-needy" all night, and it seemed the more she drank, the less she thought his comments were humorous.

"Paul, let's get it straight—you're obviously the needy one that hits on every girl to no avail and loves to make fun of others for attention. How many of these girls have you coerced to kiss you, yet none of them want to date you? Maybe you should look in the mirror to figure it out."

Samantha cringed when she heard this. Jenni was obviously callous enough to hit below the belt when she felt at odds with someone. Sam perceived a sense of foreboding when she heard Jenni strike back in such a caustic way. She didn't understand people who resorted in exerting words that couldn't be taken back, who strike at such a personal level. It commonly didn't end well.

"No, I make fun of you because I don't like you, and I'm not sure if you get that being able to kiss girls and not have to date them is not a bad thing," Paul said half-mockingly to Jenni.

The others laughed, and Jenni looked askance at her husband and Cassandra.

"Oh, do you think that's funny, Cass? Why don't you find a husband of your own to flirt with?"

"Whoa, how did I get in the middle of the fire?" Cass questioned Jenni.

No one wanted to be Jenni's target when she got worked up, knowing she wouldn't be merciful on anyone.

"I see the way you fawn over him."

Cassandra stared at Jenni with her mouth agape, not knowing how to respond.

Scott then stood up. "Okay, Jenni, time to go to bed. I think you've had enough to drink."

"Oh, are you protecting your girlfriend now?" She shot back at him with fury in her eyes.

"That's enough!" Scott said with force. He grabbed her by the arm and marched her out of the room like a scolded child before she could say another word.

Megan tried to pacify the situation. "We've all had too much to drink. I think we should all call it a night."

After she said that, a bedroom door slammed shut in the distance.

Sam closed their bedroom door as Megan began to undress to put on her pajamas.

"Can you believe Jenni said that about Cass and her husband? Do you really think she believes there is something going on between them or was she just drunk and going off at the mouth?" Megan pondered the question she asked Samantha.

Due to the conversation she had with Jenni at the pool, Sam said thoughtfully, "I think she is very insecure about her relationship with her husband yet would never admit to it. I think Cassandra is just her target because she is pretty and flirtatious. I don't know, maybe she does think there's something going on, but I don't know them well enough to know if it's her own insecurities or if she has legitimate concern. What do you think?"

"Jenni is the jealous type and needs attention, but I have never heard her voice concerns about Scott's fidelity before. I'm sure it was mostly about the alcohol consumption that prompted her to react like that. You're right—Cassandra is a target because she is brazenly flirtatious. I feel bad for Scott that his own wife embarrassed him in front of everyone."

Megan opened the door to their private balcony and stepped outside to hear the sound of the waves crash against the pitch-black beach. She looked down and noticed Scott sitting alone on the main deck drinking a beer, staring out where the coast was now draped in onyx.

"I think I'm going to go see if Scott is okay. He is sitting alone on the deck," Megan said as she walked toward the bedroom door. "Sleep well."

CHAPTER 9

PAUL WAS POURING ORANGE juice into a glass when Jenni sundered into the kitchen. He looked up and commented derisively, "I'm only getting orange juice for Scott. I'm not sleeping with him. I promise."

"Ha ha, very funny, Paul." Jenni knew she made a fool out of herself last night by lashing out at Cassandra for flirting with Scott and she didn't expect anything less from Paul. Paul and she typically had a combative relationship, but she decided she wanted to make nice with him because she had other things more perplexing in her life that she wanted to focus on. She didn't want to be sidetracked by the constant embroilment that was the nature of their relationship. "You know, Paul, you actually are a funny guy. I may have overacted last night. I think it had to do with the booze."

"Not everyone can be as charming and witty while drinking… or when sober." Paul brushed off her weak attempt of an apology with humor.

"I can see why women are drawn to you…"

He looked at her skeptically. "Because of my dashing movie-star looks and my awesomely huge pecs?" Paul interrupted Jenni's thought.

"Um," Jenni treaded lightly, knowing he was kidding yet not wanting to disagree. "Because of your fantastically dry sense of humor." Jenni smiled sweetly at Paul. "It does seem like Misty thinks you're all that and a bag of chips."

"I prefer to be *Baked Lays*. I'm watching my weight."

Jenni dismissed this comedic retort because truthfully, she really found Paul's humor banal. She was trying to get back in his good graces—or at least the mediocre medium they're used to.

"She's a really sweet girl, but I think you can do better."

Jenni was trying to sweet-talk him after her episode last night, but the only way she knew how to do that was by insulting someone else. He found her attempt pitiful.

"She could probably do better than me. I'm a short dude with a gut—every girl's dream man." Paul tried to belittle himself in an attempt to discourage Jenni from talking bad about Misty, but Jenni didn't deduce his purpose.

Meanwhile, Misty was making her way to breakfast while this conversation was going on, and before she rounded the corner to the kitchen, the mention of her name made her halt.

Jenni's voice drifted. "Let's face it—Misty isn't going to win any beauty contest. She'd be lucky to get a short guy with a gut. I feel sorry for her because we all know that when everyone says she has such a great personality it's because she isn't pretty."

Misty was briefly paralyzed by the spiteful words she heard coming from the kitchen. She knew the hurtful words came from Jenni's mouth. She felt disheartened and appalled that Jenni spoke of her with such contempt. Tears welled up in her eyes, and she hurried back upstairs. She was embarrassed by her adverse reaction because she thought she was done with caring about how others viewed her. She didn't want to be that weak little girl being picked on at school and crying instead of sticking up for herself. She had gone to a lot of therapy to not have her past emotional baggage cripple her any more. She was disappointed in how those words still affected her deeply, and she didn't want Paul and Jenni to know she heard what was said.

Paul knew that Jenni's intent was to flatter Paul and deem herself more desirable, but she hadn't learned it just made her less attractive and mean.

He rolled his eyes. "Sometimes it's better to be known as sweet then wear a fucking crown," and grabbed the glasses of orange juice and headed to the deck where the others were sitting eating breakfast.

On her way down to get breakfast, Samantha passed Misty in the hall and saw she was visibly upset, "Misty, are you okay?"

Misty immediately put a smile on her face and said, "Hi, Sam. Yes, I'm fine, thanks for asking. I forgot something in my room."

Sam didn't believe Misty but figured if she wanted to discuss why she's distressed, she would.

Samantha headed out to the deck where everyone was sitting around eating breakfast and talking. It looked like everyone was on amicable terms and in good spirits. Jenni was sitting on her husband's lap with her arm draped around his neck. Either they made up last night or she was letting everyone know this was her property and putting on the semblance that once again everything was wonderful in their marriage.

Cassandra greeted Samantha, "Morning, Sam, do you have anything planned today? Some of us are going to head to one of the public beaches to check out the action if you want to come."

"Thanks, I would, but I'm going to hook up with one of my high school friends, and we're going to hit the outlets and then we'll probably come back here and lie by the pool, if no one minds."

"That's totally cool. I forgot you're from here. Where would be a good public beach to head today that has beach volleyball and a good scene?"

"Gosh, I haven't lived here in ages, but back in my day, a lot of people would go to the beach behind the Back Porch, it's a restaurant. There are volleyball nets, and it used to always be a fun time. Then you can grab lunch there too. Or if you want to head into Fort Walton, there's the Boardwalk that has restaurants overlooking the beach and several volleyball nets. The restaurant the Crab Trap is there and is very good. There's a Crap Trap right down the road also, but the boardwalk is where I used to go and worked one summer. The Gulfarium is also there, but honestly, I've never even been there, and I lived in Fort Walton. If y'all are thinking about charting a deep-sea fishing boat one day this week, I think it's by AJ's and the Lucky Snapper. I used to work at the Lucky Snapper also, but I'm not sure if it's still there, now that I think about it."

"Thanks for the suggestions. Let us know how the outlets are and if there are any great deals. I know I want to head there myself at one point," Cass smiled at Sam.

Looking around, she asked the group, "Has anyone seen Misty? I thought she'd be down here by now?"

Samantha looked concerned and told Cassandra, "I passed her in the hall upstairs. She looked a little disconcerted. I thought she had already been downstairs since she was heading toward her room. She said she forgot something. I asked her if she was okay. She said she was fine, but she was a little flushed and looked troubled."

Cassandra stood up and pushed back her chair and grabbed her plate and glass. "I'll go check on her."

Paul peered over at Jenni to see if she had the same notion that maybe she heard the invective comments Jenni made toward Misty. Yet Jenni continued to paw her husband and took no heed over what was being said about Misty. Grimacing, Paul thought that Jenni didn't care if someone's feelings got hurt from something she said. She was so egocentric that she was oblivious to anyone else's feelings but her own.

Just then, Kari and Justin emerged from the French doors leading onto the patio, adorned in their biking gear. Their skin was glistening from the vigorous exertion of riding their bikes, and their hair was matted to their scalps dampened by sweat. It was easy to forget that these two were even there at times since Justin wasn't a drinker, and he tended to blend into the background while the others were a lot more gregarious, especially when they drank. Plus, Kari and Justin went to bed early the night before and fortunately missed all the intoxicated drama between Jenni and Paul, Jenni and Cassandra, and Jenni and her own husband. But looking at Jenni perched on Scott's lap, no one would ever fathom that there were harsh words the night before.

Jenni turned toward her friend. "Wow, y'all need a shower."

Kari was standing on the deck, holding her bicycle helmet in the crotch of her arm with Justin standing behind her diffidently. She laughed at Jenni's rudeness. "Jeez, Jenni, you're so observant... and you haven't even smelled us yet."

Jenni sneered, "I can imagine. We're heading out around eleven and *you're* coming with us. You went to bed way too early last night, and we didn't get to hang. We're going to the beach and may go explore a little, have lunch, what not."

Kari reached her hand behind her to grab Justin's hand. "*We'll* join you guys. We're going to grab some breakfast, take a shower and we'll be ready to go." Kari turned to head to the kitchen, still holding Justin's hand, as Justin timidly waved to everyone and followed Kari inside.

Jenni watched as the two disappeared inside the house and snorted, "Ugh, I wish she didn't bring him. She's so much more fun without him."

"Babe, that *is* her boyfriend. You better get used to it," Scott told his wife.

Jenni smiled sweetly to Scott and said, "You're right, sweetie." She raised her hand to caress his face and purred, "Let's go take a walk on the beach to get some exercise."

"Ah, honey, I totally would but Chris and I are going for a run on the beach in a few. You're welcome to come too… if you can keep up."

A look of disappointment washed over Jenni's face but she quickly smiled. "Oh, okay that's fine. Megan, do you and Samantha feel like taking a walk on the beach?"

Megan and Sam looked at each other hesitantly, then Megan said, "Sure, why not. We could all use some exercise." It's hard for Megan to say no to anyone especially when others were listening.

"I would, but my friend is coming over soon to head to the outlets, and I don't want to be all sweaty to try on clothes. But next time, I'm in," Sam told Jenni.

Sam got up to go inside to get ready and whispered sarcastically to Megan as she passed her. "Have fun."

Misty and Cassandra emerged from the inside of the house, and Megan immediately recruited them to go with her and Jenni on the walk. Although the last thing Misty wanted was to be around Jenni after her remarks, she didn't want anyone to know how upset and angry she was at Jenni.

Megan was relieved they agreed to go. She didn't want to plaster a smile to her face as Jenni went on and on about herself and hear specifics of why her marriage with Scott was so great when it would be such a farce. She tolerated Jenni, but on a one-to-one basis, she would rather not.

On the way to her room, Samantha overheard Kari grumbling to Justin while they ate their breakfast at the breakfast nook.

"I know I shouldn't get all worked up if you don't care, but she makes me so mad when she devalues our relationship by ignoring you completely. She better wise up. I'm her only true friend here, and she's on the verge of losing my alliance if she keeps it up."

Samantha knew exactly who Kari was referring to when she heard her grievance.

"Scott should really keep her in line better."

Samantha was surprised to hear Justin's chauvinistic answer to controlling Jenni's behavior, but she reasoned, he did work in a male-dominant, testosterone-filled environment. They're more prone to have those types of gender views.

After only being at the beach house one night, and Jenni already had most of the guests unhappy with her attitude. Sam wondered if she should feel sorry for Jenni because of the underlining issues that were the culprit of her behavior, or was Samantha being the consummate therapist drawing conclusions and excuses for someone who just may be a self-centered egotist? She didn't really want to give it much thought. She was on vacation, wasn't she?

CHAPTER 10

THE DOORBELL RANG AND Samantha went to greet her friend, Mia. She was supposed to be there around the time the others left for the beach, but as usual, Mia was late.

"Wow, girl, this house is amazing."

Sam hugged her friend and led her inside to check out the rest of the house.

"Where is everyone else?" Mia asked, looking around admiring the vastness of the rooms.

"Well, if you would have been here when you said, you could have met everyone." Sam gave her longtime friend a hard time about being late.

"How long have you known me and when am I ever on time?"

Sam playfully rolled her eyes at Mia. "They wanted to find more action than the private beach behind the house. I told them to go behind the Back Porch. I've been gone too long that I have no idea if some things are even in Destin anymore."

"Oh, okay. The Back Porch is still there. This is a nice getup you have going here," she said as she walked over to the windows that overlooked the pool and the white sandy beach with the endless blue-green water. "Let's head to the outlets so we can get back and enjoy the scenery. Oh, and we're taking your convertible."

At the beach, Justin rented an umbrella to sit under while the others unloaded their stuff around him. He enjoyed being outdoors but had to protect his pallid complexion. There were volleyball games

49

going on, and Jenni immediately went to see if she could join in. She played in high school and never shied away from asking to join a game and teaming up with whoever was playing at the beach. She and Chris jumped into one of the existing games.

Megan pulled out her oversized towel and spread it out around her. She removed her book and some trash magazines that were a staple for the beach and set them on her towel to read. She reached back in her bag to retrieve her phone and couldn't find it. She frantically searched her bag by dumping out all its contents on her towel to no avail—her phone wasn't in there.

"Shit! I'm expecting a call from work that I have to take and I must have left my phone back at the house. Shit. I need it. Oh my god, what am I going to do?"

"Meg, calm down. You can take my car back to the house to get it. It's right down the street," Scott soothed her.

"I'm horrible with directions, and I hate driving in an unfamiliar town."

"Okay, I'll drive you back. It's not a big deal. We worked together, so I know what's required, and I wouldn't want you to get in trouble."

"Really? Thank you so much, Scott. I'll totally owe you."

Samantha got behind her wheel to drive to the outlets, and Mia commented, "I haven't been in a convertible in a long time, and I live in Florida. Something is the matter with that sentence."

"Yes, there is. It's a perfect day for it too. Oh, and I brought some old CDs and here's one especially for you." Samantha grinned excitedly at her longtime friend and took out her Depeche Mode CD and put it in the disc changer and preset it to the song "Personal Jesus." Looking at her friend expectedly when the two chimes in the beginning of the song sounded, Mia knew instantly which song it was, and they both sang together, "Reach out and touch faith."

This song was their jam back in the day when they used to go to Cash's Faux Pas as underage teenagers on Okaloosa Island. Cash's was a dance club in Fort Walton Beach that was infamous for letting underage teenagers in as long as they could produce a fake ID. If you befriended the bouncers and flirted with them, they weren't too picky about the ID as long as it said you were eighteen years old. Mia had been a pro at charming the bouncers and making them feel like they were the most interesting guys around. On several occasions, Mia would show the ID she was using to the bouncer and then she'd pass it back through the line for Sam to use. This was considered a rite of passage living in a tourist town and harmless fun.

"Remember that dude, Joe, who would dance on stage like he owned the place, and this was his favorite song to act like he was so sexy."

They both put one hand behind their head and imitated the way he'd dance while he'd look down at the crowd, trying to seduce one of the young patrons, and they both laughed at each other.

"Damn it." Sam slammed on her breaks. "Stupid dumb ass." Her road rage came out again.

"It was that white Audi that almost caused an accident," Mia observed.

"That's Scott's car. He's one of the people staying in the house and it looked like Megan was in the car with him. That's strange. Figures it's an Atlanta driver causing havoc. I wonder why they're heading back to the house."

"Shit, it's not just Atlanta drivers. You haven't lived here in a long time, and the traffic is not like it was when we were growing up when Destin was barely a blimp on the map. I don't like to get out and drive when it's tourist season. It gets to be gridlock on 98 now that everyone, and their sisters come down here to vacation," Mia explained to Samantha.

"My, have things changed. We used to live for tourist season. We couldn't wait till all the different colleges would be let out for spring break and pollute our beaches with all their coolers filled with beer and their kegs buried in the sand."

"Those were the days, for sure!" Mia exclaimed.

"We're getting old, Mia, when now all we care about is that they better pick up all their trash off the beach when they leave."

"Ha, ain't that the truth. What happened to us? What happened to our semi-private paradise?"

"We should have known Destin would blow up. Destin was like a secret haven waiting to be discovered. Too bad we were kids and had no money, or else I would have invested in some real estate."

"True, but I still don't have any money. What money I have I'll invest in some shopping." Mia said as she cranked the stereo.

CHAPTER 11

SAMANTHA AND MIA HAD much success at the outlets. They were now drinking a beer and tanning by the pool. Mia was the type of friend that Sam didn't have to talk to often, and the relationship still had the same bond as years ago. This kind of bond was usually more prevalent in relationships with people who grew up together or were close in high school. It's the whole coming-of-age bond, an epoch where your friends mean the world to you because you can't relate to your parents or any other adult. It's a period of life where your world revolved around the activities of your friend's lives. It's the exploration of testing out boundaries and limits together, the confiding in secret desires, and the supportive or critical advice that seemed so detrimental in your affairs of the heart. This crucial time was what made up the attachment that carried over decades, even without a current active role in each other's lives.

Sam was telling Mia about her relationship and the ending of it in depth. Inevitably, the tears welled up in her eyes as she discussed how sad and alone she felt without Brad in her life. She admitted she never truly felt happy anymore, and she felt lost without him. Her confusion of what her relationship really meant to Brad and the disillusionment of what she thought she had constantly pried in her mind.

Mia took a swig of her beer, and thoughtfully said, "Sam, marriage is a lot of hard work and not always fun. The grass isn't always greener. I got two great kids from my marriage but the majority of the time it was a pain in the ass. If this Brad dude can't see what an asset you'd be in his life—well then, it's his loss. If you're not wanting kids, then you're better off not getting married. He sounds like a selfish asshole."

"You're not the first person to tell me this. But it wasn't really about getting married. We lived too far apart and I wanted to see him more. We had a great relationship… or so I thought. What kills me is I still think he loves me, but logically if he did, we'd be together. I've always had too big of an ego to believe someone wouldn't want to be with me on their own accord. I tend to blame extenuating circumstances for the demise of the relationship instead of seeing it in black and white. I definitely need to work on that. I just can't seem to shake him. I miss him every day. I liked having someone who I felt had my back and who told me he loved me. He was my best friend." Samantha's voice cracked when she talked about Brad and she felt a strain in her chest.

"He's not an asshole." Sam still felt the need to defend him.

"He doesn't sound that nice to me—from what you've told me, he sounds like a big pussy. Do you really want a big pussy, someone that doesn't deal well under pressure, who runs from a hard time? Life can be a hard time, and you don't want…" Mia's voice trailed off, she was looking past Samantha, and a huge smile formed on her face. "Hey, Bubba, what the hell are you doing here?"

Sam turned in her lounge chair and saw a bronzed, distinguished, older man with sun-bleached hair walking up the private boardwalk toward the pool. She wiped away her tears and put her sunglasses back on, so he wouldn't know she had been crying.

"Hey, Mia, I was out in my driveway when I saw you pass in a convertible. I live right next door. I knocked at the front door, but figured you must be out by the pool when no one answered."

Mia was born and raised in Fort Walton Beach and she never left to go away to college so she knew a lot of people in this town. Samantha wasn't surprised at this chance meeting.

"Bubba, this is my good friend Samantha, who is down with some friends from Atlanta."

Mia looked at Sam. "Bubba owns the yacht that Jeff captains."
Jeff was Mia's ex-boyfriend.

"Oh, okay. Nice to meet you."

"Likewise," Bubba said to Sam as he extended his hand to recognize her.

"I came over here to invite you girls and whoever else is staying here to my party tomorrow night. I'm going to have a band, plenty of bars. It should be pretty wild and crazy."

"We'll be there," Mia answered for Sam. "Bubba throws amazing parties, and *wild* and *crazy* is exactly the right words to use to describe them. This girl here could use a little wild and crazy." She pointed at Sam when she said this.

"Is that a fact? Why, are you shy and reserved?" Bubba asked Sam.

Mia chided Bubba before Sam could speak. "Hell, no. She's dealing with a broken heart, and she needs some fun in her life."

"I'm sorry to hear that. I learned a long time ago that life is much too short to worry about someone who isn't spending any of their time thinking of you. Besides, you're too pretty to be single long. There will be a lot of eligible men at the party who will be honored to get to spend time and have a laugh with you."

Mia looked anxious for a moment and asked Bubba, "Wait, is Jeff going to be there?"

"You're in luck, sweetheart. Jeff is on his way down to Miami with the boat. I needed him to take it down there and drop it off, and I didn't have the time to go with him."

"Yep, then we're there," Mia said, relieved her ex wouldn't be around.

"There are eight other people staying in this house." Sam prudently told Bubba to give him a heads-up when a big group of people showed up to his party.

Bubba grinned sweetly at Sam. "Darling, my motto is 'The more, the merrier.' In fact, if you want to bring anyone else, feel free."

Mia wasn't quite sure how Bubba made his millions. She knew he came from money but also that he was a savvy businessman. In fact, she only knew him from social settings when he'd invited her and her ex to parties on the yacht or at restaurants. All she really knew was he paid for everything and he knew how to have a good time. He was in his early fifties, and was a great-looking man who maintained his trim and toned physique. He never lacked a bevy of beautiful women kowtowing to his every need.

"Bubba, can we offer you a beer?" Samantha felt compelled to ask after his generous invitation to attend his party.

"Darling, I would love nothing more than to sit and chat with you beautiful girls and have a drink, but I have guests at my house." He grabbed both their hands and kissed them. "I look forward to seeing you both tomorrow around eight."

Sam noticed that Bubba was a charmer but thought to herself, *Aren't most single, attractive, older, rich men usually pretty suave when it comes to talking to the ladies?*

Watching Bubba saunter over the boardwalk toward the beach, Mia smiled at Sam. "There's a guy for ya. He's rich, good-looking, and throws a great party. Of course, you'd be one of many, but that might not be so bad if he took you on exotic trips and bought you things."

"Really? You'd date a fifty-some-year-old for money?"

"Hell yes—we're knocking on forty's door. Plus, he's a good-looking older gentleman… with money. There are exceptions to be made."

"Maybe, if he wasn't such a playboy. I'm not interested in a man who is trying too hard to hold on to his youth and uses his wealth as a way to date a multitude of different women."

"He was married before and has kids. I don't think he feels the need to do it again."

"Forget it, that's exactly the type I want to run from. That's the conclusion Brad came to with our relationship—not knowing if he ever wants to marry again. I don't want to willingly go down that path again!"

"What path is that?" Megan asked as she and Chris appeared on the pool deck, surprising Mia and Sam.

Sam let out a startled gasp. "Lord, I didn't hear you guys come out here." She made the introductions to Mia.

"The beach was really hot. We decided to come back here to hang at the pool. Kari and Justin came back too. I think Kari is coming out, but I think Justin has had enough sun."

"I'm going to make some cocktails. Who wants a drink?" Chris, the enduring bartender, asked the women.

They all chimed in to make a pitcher of something refreshing.

"I'll help you carry the glasses. Plus, we bought some snacks. I'll bring them out for us," Mia volunteered as she followed Chris inside.

Megan and Sam both looked at each other knowingly, thinking the same thing.

"Do you think she likes him?"

"Knowing Mia, yes. She isn't one to pop right up to help serve others—it's usually the other way around."

They both heard the sliding glass door open and saw Kari and Justin step through the doorway heading toward them. Justin only had on a tiny black Speedo and goggles around his head with the lenses placed on his forehead so he could see. He was whiter than usual because he had lathered his entire body in protective sunscreen.

"Justin is heading out to swim in the gulf. Since he was accepted to try out for the Green Berets, he has to work hard to get ready for their training," Kari explained to Sam and Megan after she noticed both their eyes opened wide staring at Justin's tiny swimsuit.

Justin coyly waved as he passed them and headed toward the beach.

"Go, girl, your man has a nice physique!" Megan observed, smiling at Kari.

"Ha! Yeah, he's not too bad, is he? Considering how often he works out, he better look like that."

"It's pretty impressive that he was accepted by the Green Berets. He must be very excited to have the opportunity," Sam commented.

"It's been a tough road, to be honest. He originally applied to the Navy Seals, but he didn't pass the interview. He was really distressed about the whole situation."

"What happened with the interview?" Sam inquired.

"Well, he wasn't totally forthcoming about it, but he mentioned that they asked about his ex-wife. He said because he got visually upset about a question they asked about their divorce that something like that could ruin his chances. He said they expect you to be stoic and strong about every aspect of your life. Supposedly, you can't show any vulnerability or they think you won't be able to hack being a Navy Seal."

"Wow, really? That's interesting. I can kind of understand that reasoning because the Special Forces need people that are not only of sound body but are of sound mind. The interviewer is probably trained to be hypersensitive to any display of emotional distress since once a candidate is accepted, they have to deal with seeing stuff that most would deem traumatizing," the counselor side of Sam responded.

Megan ignored that aspect of the interview and asked, "Did you ask what the question was that got him emotional about his ex?"

Candidly, Kari told them, "Well, he told me his relationship with his ex-wife was volatile. She sounded crazy and would pick fights with him. She was eight years older and was insecure, and she played off his youth and naivety. She called the cops during one of their disputes, and even though I don't think any charges were filed, the military has a way of knowing things, and they asked something about it. He told me he was a little rattled and got upset knowing something as trivial as a stupid fight with his ex-wife could ruin his chance of becoming a Navy Seal. And apparently, it did."

"Yet the Green Berets didn't have a problem with it?" Sam inquired.

"I guess not. I'm not sure if they even asked the same questions. They're two different branches of the military, so I'm assuming two different methods of picking their men. He's a pretty mild-mannered guy, as I'm sure you've noticed, but he is crazy athletic and has an intensity that apparently the Green Berets found desirable."

Samantha found Kari's candor refreshing. She had a great sense of humor and portrayed herself with realness, with no pretenses. She was the type of girl that spoke her mind and had a toughness about her, yet there was a kindness that was emoted through her hazel eyes. She had that unique quality that a lot of guys say they are looking for, a girl who is down to earth and someone who would do athletic adventures but also a lady that could dress up and be comfortable in heels. Justin should consider himself a lucky guy, Sam thought to herself.

In the kitchen, Mia was searching the cupboards for plastic bowls for the tortilla chips and the salsa. She was heating up some cheese in the microwave, and Chris was deciding which liquors he would mix for a tasty drink.

They had been making small talk when Mia decided to find out if Chris was single. "Are you and Megan dating?"

"No, we're just friends. I'm just friends with all these women but I did have a crush on Jenni and we went out a handful of times... but she's married to Scott now."

"Hmm..." Mia thought that was a curious confession—was he telling her that because he wasn't interested in her? "Does that upset you that she's married now?"

"Oh, no, no, I was just answering your question with a little too much information." He nervously chuckled. "It was a long time ago when I took her out. I thought she was very pretty, but she obviously didn't see anything in me. I thought we had a good time on our dates. I guess I wasn't good-enough-looking for what she was ultimately looking for. Although she can be selfish and disagreeable at times, I would have treated her like gold. I mean, she married a great guy, but she still expects me to cater to her. I guess I don't mind since we've remained friends and she will confide in me about personal things."

Mia just shook her head acting like she understood because she really didn't know how to respond.

"Ugh, I went on and on again, didn't I? I think I'm a little nervous because I think you're very attractive."

"Aw, sweet."

Mia found his self-deprecating style cute and endearing, but she detected some bitterness in Chris's recollection of his time spent with Jenni. Sam did say Jenni didn't have the greatest bedside manner, so she didn't scrutinize it too much. Besides, she thought Chris was adorable, and she didn't really care about his past heartaches. She lived in Fort Walton and he lived in Atlanta; she wasn't looking to date the guy.

Mia and Chris walked out to the pool area, balancing two trays of snacks and a pitcher full of watermelon-infused vodka, lemonade-flavored Crystal Light, and Bacardi.

"Chris, looks like you're one of the girls this afternoon."

Chris looked from Sam to Mia, Megan, and Kari and smiled. "I like my odds!"

Kari grabbed a cup and poured a drink. "I'm ready to drink and have some fun. What's the plan tonight?"

Kari hadn't had a drink since she'd been in Destin on account of Justin not partaking, but she was geared up to ingest the tasty mixture while Justin swam in the gulf.

"I made a reservation for dinner at a place called AJ's. It's just a fun, casual restaurant that has good seafood, and it's on the water. After dinner, we can head upstairs to the bar that overlooks the harbor and boats that are docked there. They have live music, and it gets pretty packed in there. The clientele is usually pretty eclectic. You have young twenty-somethings to older patrons to fishheads. I haven't been in a long time, but it's always been a good time," Sam explained to the group.

"What the hell is a fishhead?" Kari asked mockingly.

Sam and Mia looked at each other and laughed. Growing up in a beach town, the word *fishhead* is a commonly used term to describe certain people.

"Fishheads are the guys that work out on the boats all day. You'll be able to spot them. They're the men with the deep dark tans with a stripe of white across their temples and the bridge of their noses where their sunglasses cover, and if they took off their watch it would match those white marks. They are always in flip-flops, shorts, and a T-shirt. They usually have ball caps or visors on, and their Costa sunglasses are normally hanging from a strap around their necks."

"Well, okay then, bring on the fishheads!" Kari said as she put her cup up to cheers.

The women clinked cups and agreed, "Bring on the fishheads!"

Later on, in the late afternoon, everyone was home either resting, taking showers to get ready for the night, or lounging by the pool or at the beach. Samantha and Megan were in their bedroom, contemplating what to wear to dinner. Samantha had the door open to their personal porch facing the beach to enjoy the sun slowly setting behind the water. She stepped outside to revel in the orange, red, and yellow mottled brilliance of the sun against the light-blue background, knowing how quickly it would disappear in the horizon.

Looking down, she saw Misty and Paul sitting by the pool relaxing. She spotted Scott and Cassandra down at the beach in the water with two boogie boards trying to catch a wave and ride it in. It looked like a lot of fun, and she commented to Megan that they should try to do it tomorrow. Megan dropped her dress and rushed outside to witness Scott and Cassandra in the wake.

"Are you that curious about boogie boarding, or are you hoping to catch them doing something illicit?"

Megan felt foolish for her overly curious behavior and laughed it off. "Yep, I guess I'm like most people and want to gawk at something that might be scandalous."

"You know him pretty well and always talk about what a great guy he is. You don't think he would cheat on his wife, do you?"

"If I were him, I'd cheat on her."

"He knew who he was marrying."

"I guess you're right." Megan looked back at the two of them in the Gulf. Just then Justin and Kari walked out to the beach. Kari dropped her cover-up and ran to the water. Cassandra handed her the board and headed to the shore. She wrapped herself in a towel and sat in the sand next to Justin. Scott was in the water, demonstrating to Kari how she should paddle and kick to catch a wave.

Megan commented to Samantha, "It looks innocent enough. I'm getting in the shower. Maybe we can find some drama tonight."

Paul was reclined in the lounge chair by the pool, feeling at ease with Misty beside him. She was a laid-back girl who thought his sense of humor was clever and entertaining. He enjoyed her company as well. She asked him what he thought about Jenni's antics last night and the brutal things she had said to him. Paul shrugged it off and told her that he did not lose sleep over it.

She confessed that she wished she could have the same outlook as he when it came to Jenni because she had overheard her in the kitchen this morning insulting her and it still bothered her. She wished she could just let it go, but it kept boiling to the surface every time she was in the same room with her. She explained she was not the type of person to make a scene and she was able to keep her emotions in check around her, but in reality, she thought about piercing her through the eyeball with a fork.

Paul felt bad that Misty had heard the cruel things Jenni said about her. He explained to her that this was just the type of person Jenni was and he paid her no attention. But as far as wanting to fork her eyeballs out, Paul told her to get in line.

Inside, Jenni and Chris were sitting on the living room sofa while Jenni inundated him with all the distress in her life. Jenni knew she'd have Chris's undivided attention, and lately, she'd felt a lack of that from her husband. She knowingly manipulated Chris's attraction for her to satisfy her ego. She casually placed her hand on his thigh as she relayed the anguish she had experienced from different events in her life lately. She didn't confess to Chris that she anticipated Scott may be having an affair, but she did tell him that she'd been feeling neglected by him, hoping that Chris would be extra sensitive and diligent to her needs this week.

Paul and Misty walked inside, and Paul noticed Jenni and Chris cuddled up on the couch conversing. Immediately he felt defensive because he knew Jenni had beguiled Chris with the erroneous certitude that she found him attractive and he was important in her life. Whenever the group went out together, Chris acted oblivious to Jenni's guileful maneuvers to distract him every time he was hitting on woman. It was infuriating to Paul when his best friend was essentially being cock-blocked by a woman he had no chance of ever being with. Paul was almost certain Jenni would behave as some sort of obstacle to hinder Mia from getting close to Chris tonight.

"Chris, Mia is a hot piece of ass, and she was digging you, man. You need to take her home tonight. She looks like a wild one that gives good head." Paul tried to provoke backlash from Jenni while reminding Chris that there was an available girl going out tonight who happened to be interested in him.

"Ugh, grow up!" Jenni abruptly got up from the couch and walked out of the room. That was precisely the reaction he had been hoping for.

"Bye, Jenni," Paul said under his breath as she left the room.

CHAPTER 12

DINNER TURNED OUT TO be a blithe occasion for the group. They lingered over cocktails and appetizers and took turns retelling laughable stories of past events. They were seated at one of the picturesque windows facing the harbor where they could see the yachts pulling in to dock and envy the people having cocktails on the ones already stationed. After dinner, they headed upstairs to the rooftop bar.

The bar was reverberating with the animated sounds of live music, laughter, and the indistinguishable chatter of conversing customers. The atmosphere gave way to an electric and lively mood. In the center of the room stood the huge main bar surrounded by a superfluous amount of people occupying all the stools around the bar or standing talking to the lucky ones who managed to find a seat. The bar was covered by a thatched roof supported by wooden posts defaced by the profusely inscribed signatures collected from the multitude of vacationers who stopped by. There were plastic parrots and toucans scattered throughout the space to give it a more tropical vibe.

The group wandered around the bar, looking for any unoccupied tables to claim. Cassandra spotted a couple of guys standing, looking like they were getting up to leave on the farthest deck. The posse of men were about to abandon their table as they threw cash out for a tip. Cassandra raced over to grab the table before anyone else could get there first.

She smiled sweetly at the men and said, "Just grabbing your table before anyone else does," as she sat seductively crossing her legs on one of the empty stools.

"If we knew you were here, we wouldn't be leaving," one of the men flirted back with her.

Cassandra giggled demurely. "Have a good night, boys!"

The others gathered around the table.

"Cass, keep on your panties. We just got here," Paul harassed her.

"Don't be jealous, Paul." Cassandra winked at him.

"She can't help it that she's a dude magnet," Scott chimed in.

She flashed her brilliantly white smile at Scott and asked, "Who wants to go dance?"

Sam, Mia, Chris, and Paul stayed behind to make sure no one took their confiscated table. The conversation turned to the topic of Misty having a crush on Paul. Paul bypassed their inquiries of his feelings for her but told them that Samantha was right about Misty being upset when she ran into her in the hall before breakfast.

Paul explained, "I was concerned when you said Misty looked visually upset this morning because prior to that, Jenni and I were in the kitchen talking about her. Well, not exactly talking about her— Jenni brought her name up. She was trying to butter me up from being a total evil bitch to me the night before. She tried compliment-ing me by telling me I could do better than Misty and how Misty wasn't pretty... just stupid shit. I thought I heard someone coming around the corner, but no one appeared, so I thought I was wrong. Apparently, it was Misty. She said she had heard Jenni comment on her appearance. She confided in me about how she felt really embar-rassed and humiliated that Jenni would say those kinds of things about her. Misty is a true sweetheart, but you don't want to get on her bad side. She had venom in her eyes when talking about Jenni. It was kind of scary because I don't know that side of Misty. She mentioned being teased growing up, and I think Jenni's comments really struck a chord with her and made her regress back to those unfavorable times in her life. But she hasn't said anything to Jenni or been overly rude to her. You know how you women are—you talk bad about each other but then act like best friends to each other's faces. Jenni better not press her luck with Misty or she may end up face down in the pool, ha! Isn't it always the sweet, innocent-looking ones that are the most threatening and nuts?"

"That sounds like just the type of girl you're looking for." Chris poked his friend.

"Yeah, I'll take it in the bedroom but not looking for a bunny boiler."

Sam ignored Paul's last comment. "Oh, that's sad she had to hear something like that when she's such a sweet girl. Past experiences can be very detrimental in the way we perceive ourselves today and can trigger a tremendous amount of insecurity and anger. That's unfortunate that she is insecure about her looks when she has such a warm and funny personality." Sam expressed her sympathy for Misty.

"Sam, saying she has a warm and funny personality is equivalent to saying she's a dog but just in a nicer way. It's like telling a fat person they have a pretty face," Mia told her friend in an apathetic tone.

"You're a mess," Sam laughed. "I think Misty is attractive, and it's more of a plus that she's a cool chick."

"You should sleep with her tonight to make her feel pretty," Chris laughingly told Paul. Mia laughed along with Chris.

"That always makes me feel pretty," Mia said as she glanced up seductively at Chris.

Sam rolled her eyes at her friend. "Please do not sleep with that poor girl unless you want something more. That is *not* the way to make an insecure woman feel better about herself. That's how you get a bunny boiler."

"I'm not that much of a dick. Unless she was throwing herself at me." He glanced sideways at Mia, referring to her suggestive comment she made to Chris. "I'm not going to do that to a nice girl who is into me. I'd take her to dinner a couple times, and *then* sleep with her, and by then, she won't want to date *me*." Paul grinned.

Paul got up from his seat when he saw Justin coming back to the table. "Where's Kari? Are you done dancing?"

"Yes, I'm finished. Kari's still out on the dance floor singing to the band, having fun. I may call it a night soon."

Since Justin didn't drink, Paul wasn't too surprised that this environment probably wasn't Justin's cup of tea.

"I hear ya, dude." Paul patted Justin on his back as he offered him his seat. "I think I'll head out there and embarrass the girls with my amazing dance moves."

Shortly after, Kari and Megan stumbled back to the table. Since there was a limited number of chairs, Sam pried Mia away from Chris to do what they used to call a drive-by. This is what Sam and Mia termed walking around a bar to locate people they may know, seeking out men they found good-looking to either make eye contact with or talk to, or just passing by men who offered to buy a drink—a "drive-by."

They didn't even make it halfway around the bar when Sam spotted a tall, blue-eyed, dark-haired man standing in front of her path, grinning at her.

Sam turned to Mia and exclaimed, "Look who it is—Jake 'the Cowboy' Johnson."

CHAPTER 13

SAMANTHA HAD HAD A schoolgirl crush on Jake when she was in the ninth grade and he was a big senior. Jake was popular, a football player and handsome. Sam still remembered distinctively when he had first flirted with her one day while she was hanging football posters in the hall at school. Mia and Sam were wearing their cheerleading uniforms, hanging the signs they had painted earlier that week when Jake came over to compliment their artwork. He was bold enough to come over to talk to them, yet there was a courteous quality about him. When he spoke to Sam, he displayed this sheepish grin that made him look like he was up to no good, and when he smiled, his blue eyes seemed to twinkle with a dare.

His friend came by and said, "Ladies, you are talking to Jake 'the Cowboy' Johnson." Jake looked slightly embarrassed but laughed with his friend and they both walked off together.

Samantha looked at Mia and said with earnest, "I want to take a ride on the cowboy!"

They both giggled, knowing Sam was a virgin and was just making a play on the words, but Sam was giddy from talking to him and never forgot that exchange. Sam still didn't know what the cowboy reference meant, but that title was what she thought of whenever his name came up.

After high school, Samantha and Jake had seen each other at various parties and even went out a time or two. Nothing serious ever developed between the two of them, but she always had an affinity for him. It had been years since they'd run into each other. Sam had heard he was a detective for the Okaloosa County police department. Now that Sam had had experience with helping the Atlanta police department in a couple of homicide cases, she was eager to talk with Jake about his position.

Jake saw Samantha and Mia walking toward him, and he automatically had that shit-eating grin on his face, and his baby blues danced with amusement.

"Well, hello there, pretty ladies."

He gave them both a hug and asked Samantha what she was doing in town.

Mia excused herself since she saw Jake frequently, and she wanted to get back to flirting with Chris. She knew Samantha wouldn't mind being left with Jake.

"What are you doing here all alone?" Sam inquired.

"I was working late on an assignment across the street, so I thought I'd say hi to some people who work here."

"Are you allowed to hug women while on duty?" Sam gibed Jake.

"Probably wouldn't look too good, but I'm not on duty, so you better watch out, I can do whatever I want." He flashed that sexy, confident grin again.

"Ah, let me guess... most local people know you're a cop and you stand here, and look all important while the women flock around you."

"Whatever works, darling," he said with a wink. "Actually, I came down to the docks because Jackson was weighing a huge cobia he brought in today."

Sam was assuming Jake was referring to Pete Jackson, who went to the same high school and was Jake's best friend.

"I stopped in here because I know the manager and some staff. They appreciate the work I do for the community, and because of that, they give me free hushpuppies. It's a win/win."

Samantha had to laugh. Jake was the epitome of the small-town, down-to-earth mentality that she found refreshing after living in Atlanta for so long.

Samantha described some of the work she had done with the Atlanta homicide investigative unit, and Jake seemed genuinely impressed. While Jake was relaying a story of a tourist who went missing, Sam saw over Jake's shoulder Jenni and Scott on the dance floor looking like they were having an argument. Whatever Jenni was saying, Scott didn't seem to like. He had a scowl on his face and was rolling his eyes. Scott said something back with a shrug, and Jenni turned abruptly and walked away.

Ah, the lovebirds at it again, Sam thought sarcastically. Jake drew her attention back when the missing tourist story became a homicide investigation. He concluded the story with the murderer being someone the poor girl had just met and hooked up with while out at a club.

"Kind of like that Natalee Holloway girl in Aruba, but this isn't Aruba, and we got the guy," Jake said proudly.

Samantha smiled warmly at him and nodded her head in support. "That's awesome. How did you find him?"

"That's the key about knowing a lot of people in your home town. There's usually always a witness who will talk. Enough work talk—what do you have going on tomorrow night?" Jake questioned Samantha.

"I think we're going to go to this guy's party that Mia knows, who also happens to be the neighbor of where we're staying."

"Bubba Hilder?"

"Yes! I mean, I'm not sure of his last name, but how many Bubbas can there be?"

"I'm going to that party! I was going to see if you wanted to go. That's ironic."

"How do you know this Bubba guy? You're right about knowing a lot of people, obviously. This town amazes me, how everyone knows everyone."

"Well, I'm good friends with Jeff, Mia's ex-boyfriend. I've known Bubba for a couple years now, great guy. Plus, I think people like to befriend me since I'm a cop. They think it's a way of casting a security net," Jake gave Sam a wink.

"Sounds like you're hanging out with some shifty people if they're worried about getting caught doing something shady." Sam playfully winked back at Jake.

"Ha-ha, you're adorable. You should know by now, Samantha, everybody is a little shady," Jake said, as he raised his eyebrows and smirked.

CHAPTER 14

Samantha joined Megan and Scott out on the dance floor when Jake left. They were the only two of the group still burning off the calories from dinner.

"Who was the cutie pie you were talking to?" Megan shouted to Sam above the music.

Sam smiled and leaned closer to Megan so she could hear. "He's a guy I went to high school with who is now a police detective in Destin. He is cute, isn't he? Coincidentally, he's coming to that party tomorrow night at our neighbors. I'm kind of excited to see him again."

"Why didn't he stay longer tonight?"

"He had been working all day, and he has an early morning tomorrow."

Tell him to wear his cop uniform tomorrow night. Nothing is sexier than a man in uniform," Megan said with a laugh.

At the table, Jenni was being overly sweet to Chris and a little intrusive. Mia was fuming, thinking to herself, *Isn't this bitch married? What is she trying to prove, knowing I'm sitting here interested in this man? Women! No wonder Chris still seems captivated by her, she totally leads him on.*

Mia had enough of Jenni blatantly flirting with Chris, so she cut off whatever Jenni was saying, stood up, and grabbed Chris's hand. "We've been sitting all night. Let's go out on the dance floor and let someone have our seats."

She looked at Jenni. "Here, would you like to sit? I think your husband is still out there dancing—maybe you should go dance with him. I wouldn't want my man out there dancing with another woman. Nowadays, you can't trust anybody." Mia made a point to bring up Jenni's husband, not realizing the nerve she had hit. She was trying to piss her off but also remind her she's married.

Jenni looked shocked and at a loss of words by Mia's audaciousness and just stared at her as she took one of the empty seats.

Not used to being put in your place, huh? Mia thought to herself as she pulled Chris away from the table.

"You crack me up how bold you are. It's definitely a turn-on," Chris told Mia, as he put his arm around her waist, walking to the dancefloor.

"Stick around. There's a lot more where that came from." Mia said in a provocative tone.

They sidled up to Sam, Megan, and Scott on the dance floor. Scott looked around them to see if his wife was behind them.

"What is everybody else doing?" he asked Chris.

"Sitting at the table drinking. Cassandra is over there,"—he pointed to the other side of the crowded dance floor—"dancing with some random guy. I think Justin is ready to leave."

Right then, Jenni appeared and interrupted, "A few of us are leaving. Do any of you want to leave now?" She glared at her husband.

Jenni felt insulted by Mia's comment, and she wasn't in the mood to be out anymore. She especially didn't want her husband around someone as brash as Mia.

"Do you want me to leave with you?" Scott probed his wife.

It was obvious to everyone else that Jenni was indirectly asking Scott to leave, but he was acting ignorant on purpose. He figured if she wanted him to leave, she needed to state what she really wanted him to do. He was having a good time and didn't want to go back to the house and have Jenni nag him all night.

"Scott, I'm leaving. You can do whatever you want to do." She did not want to let the others think she cared what her husband chose to do, especially after Mia's remark. She had to keep up the façade that she trusted him.

"Okay, I would go if you wanted me to, but if you don't care, then I'll stay. I love you, babe." He leaned in and kissed her cheek. She smiled faintly with her mouth, but her eyes were squinting with daggers coming out of them.

Although the thought of leaving with Jenni, knowing she was not happy with Scott's decision, didn't sound like a fun ride home. Sam was ready to leave. "I think I'm ready. Mia, I'm going to go. Are you going to stay?"

Mia looked at Chris, and he nodded that he wanted her to stay. "Yeah, I'll see you tomorrow for that party."

"Sounds like a plan. Oh, by the way, Jake 'the Cowboy' Johnson is coming to the party."

Mia gave her a knowing smile. "Giddy-up!"

After hearing Scott tell Jenni he was staying, Kari grabbed Justin's arm as the group was walking out. "Honey, you're just going home to sleep so you can wake up early to bike, right?"

Justin looked at her quizzically. "Umm, yeah."

"Do you mind if I stay also? I'm not ready to go to bed and I'm having fun."

Justin looked a little taken aback, but he knew the others were walking to the car and he didn't want them waiting for him as he had a discussion with Kari. He wasn't happy about Kari's decision and wanted to know why she'd rather stay than be with him, but he didn't want to prolong the conversation.

"Sure, that's fine."

"Great. Oh, and don't wake me in the morning when you get up. I seriously doubt I'll feel like biking tomorrow." Kari quickly kissed him and turned away to join the others on the dance floor.

Justin stood and stared for a minute and watched Kari put her arms around Megan and Scott, and he saw her tell them something as they high-fived each other like they were part of a club he wasn't included in.

Justin felt a little abandoned by Kari, and he didn't understand why she would want to hang out without him. He had been ready to leave hours ago but stayed so she could have fun. He begrudgingly left Kari and caught up with the others that were leaving.

They noticed Kari wasn't with him. Misty inquired, "Where's Kari?"

"Oh, she wanted to stay," Justin answered in a broody tone.

"Kari is staying? Good, she can watch over Scott," Jenni said, half to herself. Justin looked at her pensively.

Samantha wondered how fine Jenni and Justin really were with their partners staying at a bar without them. They both were distant and reticent walking to the car, and even Justin's usual taciturn behavior seemed to have a saturnine underlining.

She thought about Brad and their relationship and how she trusted him more than anyone. If she was put in the same scenario with Brad, how would she feel if he wanted to stay without her?

Sam always tried to put herself in the other person's position to understand their feelings on a situation. She understood why Jenni and Justin might be hurt with their partners staying at the bar. Although she had always trusted Brad and wouldn't think he'd do anything inappropriate without her, it was the point that you're on vacation together so you'd think you'd want to spend time together. *Ugh, why does every thought still go to Brad? When will I get over this? Great, now we have three dejected people going home*, Sam thought to herself.

As soon as she was seated in the car, Jenni immediately got out her phone to text Kari. "Watch over, Scott! Make sure Cass doesn't try to flirt with him. Just kidding. Have fun!" Next was a text to Scott: "Love you, babe. Be good—ha!"

Jenni's insecurities were at an all-time high with Scott. She felt like he was being distant with her, and he had been working later than usual. She hadn't caught him doing anything wrong in particular, but she had this intuition that something was amiss. She was usually a very self-assured woman who didn't obsess with feelings of insecurity, but something felt different in her marriage and she couldn't put her finger on it. She tried to mask it as much as she could, but tonight left her with a pit in her stomach. On the drive back to the beach house, she sat quietly, thinking how she could scheme a way to find out if Scott was being unfaithful to her.

CHAPTER 15

J USTIN WENT STRAIGHT TO bed when they arrived back at the
beach house. Jenni wasn't around, so everyone presumed she
headed to bed also. Paul, Misty, and Samantha were discussing
the night in the kitchen, while Paul poured a bourbon and coke for
himself and a glass of chardonnay for Misty. Sam declined any more
drinks.

"That place was super cool. Thanks for suggesting it," Paul said
to Sam. "Dinner was fantastic, and the band was awesome. I think
we all had a great time."

"Well, maybe not all of us," Misty said, referring to Justin and
Jenni.

"Jenni was fine most of the night. She's just pissed that Scott
didn't follow her back home. She expects everyone to do what she
wants to do and pouts when that doesn't happen. As for Justin, I
don't know what he considers fun… maybe if there was a treadmill
or a stationary bike in the bar to ride he would have had more fun.
I do think he's a nice guy but just different. I never trust a man that
doesn't drink," Paul said and took a sip of his bourbon.

"I don't want to be mean," Misty said in precaution, "but Jenni
acts like she needs constant attention or she's not happy."

Paul interrupted her, "Hence the name *Jen-needy*."

Misty's besotted laugh was louder than necessary. "True. I forgot
you call her that. She was shamelessly flirting with Chris just because
she knows he used to have the hots for her. It was kind of embarrass-

ing because she was doing it right in front of your friend Mia. It is obvious to everyone that Mia is interested in Chris, yet that didn't stop Jenni. She is so inconsiderate. Your friend handled it quite well, though. She totally interrupted her and took Chris by the hand and led him out to the dance floor. Paul and I had to stifle our laughs."

"Sounds like Mia," Sam said with a knowing nod.

"Then we got stuck sitting with Jenni, and she started peppering me about Cassandra. She was asking personal questions about her love life, which I found strange, but then I realized she's just jealous of Cassandra because she's pretty. For some reason, she feels threatened by Cassandra and thinks she flirts with Scott. We all know Cass flirts with everyone, and it's a given that if you're a male, Cass will probably flirt with you. Jenni knows this and has hung out with Cassandra enough to realize she's harmless. Then she started asking about my life, like she cares." Misty rolled her eyes as she said this.

She continued her slurring rant. "It was so transparent that she was only asking about my life to make it not seem strange about her taking such an interest in Cassandra's life. I've hung out with Jenni a lot in social environments and always considered her a friend, but after this weekend, she's shown her true colors."

Sam knew Misty was referring to what she had heard Jenni say about her to Paul.

"I just don't have a lot of respect for her, and it's hard for me to listen to a person that is as mean-spirited as she is. She can go to hell for all I care. I hope a wave takes her under and she never comes back up." Finishing her sentence, Misty downed the rest of her chardonnay.

Samantha knew Misty's diatribe was a factor of drinking all night and the hurt she felt from what Jenni said about her.

"Whoa, girl, tell us how you *really* feel," Paul said, trying to make light of Misty's comment.

"We call her Jen-needy for a reason. But aren't most of you girls a little on the needy side? I never met a girl who wasn't bitchy, caddy, and a complainer at times. All of you are head cases." Paul always found humor in being misogynistic.

"You know us so well," Sam said sarcastically.

Sam had enough of the grievances about Jenni and of Paul's chauvinistic remarks. "I'm heading to bed. Good night."

Samantha climbed the stairs heading to her room when she saw Jenni coming out of Cassandra and Misty's room. Jenni looked a little startled to see Sam and quickly commented that she was looking for a shirt she let Cassandra borrow but couldn't find it.

Samantha knew Jenni wasn't very happy about her husband staying at the bar and thought she'd reach out to comfort her. Jenni was getting a bad rap by most of the people in the house, and Samantha wanted to give her the benefit of the doubt.

She didn't know if Jenni would engage, but she still asked, "Jenni are you okay? I've been going through a hard time with my breakup, so I know it feels better to talk about things. If you want to talk about anything, I will listen."

Jenni basically scoffed at Sam, "I'm not one of your clients, Samantha, and I don't plan to be. I'm not going through a breakup like you did, so I have no idea what you are implying I may need to talk about. I'm married to a great man who loves me. I'm sorry you had a bad relationship, and he stopped loving you, but one day I hope you find a husband too. I'm going to bed." She turned on her heels and left Sam standing there with a befuddled look on her face.

Wow, what a little bitch. I should release Misty on her, Sam thought with a smirk.

CHAPTER 16

THE NEXT DAY SAMANTHA woke relatively early and noticed that Megan's bed wasn't slept in. She felt an initial panic that maybe something happened last night until she grabbed her cell phone and there were no missed calls. She quickly threw on gym shorts and a tank top and headed downstairs to check to make sure Megan was somewhere in the house.

As soon as she stepped out of the bedroom, Megan appeared in the hallway, heading toward their room.

"Are you just coming to bed?"

"Kind of—I fell asleep on the couch last night, but we stayed up most of the night swimming and drinking. You missed a good time. I'm surprised we didn't wake you."

"I didn't hear anything. I can sleep through most noises. Did Mia come back with Chris?" Sam asked about her friend.

"No, but Chris left with her. I guess they hit it off, huh?"

"Did you meet any cute guys after I left?"

"Not really, Cassandra was talking to a group of guys but I mainly just hung out and danced with Scott and Kari. I'm going to lie down for a little. What are you fixing to do?"

"I think I'm going to take a walk on the beach before it gets really hot."

Downstairs, Samantha poured herself some orange juice and reveled in the silent solitude of everyone else in the house sleeping. She walked over to the wall of windows overlooking the undulant water and white crystal beach. It was a clear morning with blue skies and fluffy cotton-ball clouds. She stared out to the magnificent view, and the waves put her in a trance like state, delivering a sedative emotional effect. She thought how much Brad would enjoy being there. It never failed—wherever she was and whatever she was doing, her mind drifted to Brad, and melancholy rushed over her. Even when she was having a good time, she imagined it would be better if Brad were there to experience it with her. She had tried to turn off these thoughts, but they were in her subconscious. She could be in a roomful of people engaging in interesting conversations, yet she'd feel this sense of being alone, and consciously, she knew it was because Brad was gone from her life.

If he doesn't want to be a part of my life, I should let him go. It's his loss… let go, she thought to herself resolutely. She put on her earphones and headed out to the boardwalk.

Mia pulled up to the palatial beach house and turned to Chris. "Tell Sam I'll be back tonight to go to that party." She sarcastically added, "Oh, and tell Jenni I said hi."

Chris grabbed Mia's face and kissed her. "You're so bad. I'll see you tonight. I hope the guys aren't waiting on me to go fishing."

"Have fun," Mia called out through the passenger window as Chris hurried toward the house.

Chris looked around the quiet living room and was relieved the guys weren't anxiously expecting him. He spied Paul sitting in the breakfast nook eating cereal.

Chris asked Paul, "Where is everybody else?"

"Apparently, it was a late night for Scott, but he's rallying. Justin just got back from cycling and is in the shower. We don't have to be at the boat till ten, so it's all good."

"Did someone have a good time last night or what?"

"Shit!" Chris jumped.

Jenni startled both Paul and Chris. They didn't hear her walking up behind them, and now, she was standing there, staring at them with a disapproving look.

Chris composed himself and laughed at Jenni rattling him. "Which one of us are you referring to?"

"Well, I guess both of you, since you both seem to have found girls that are enamored or, should I say, fooled by you guys. But since you're wearing the same clothes as last night," Jenni said, looking Chris up and down, "I'm guessing you didn't come home with the others and may have had the most fun... hmmm?"

"Awww." Chris put his hand on top of Jenni's head and mussed up her hair like you'd do to a little kid. "Thanks for caring about my love life, Jenni," he said sardonically.

Jenni backed up, feeling indignant from Chris touching her. "Don't flatter yourself, I really don't care. Mia is a rude, uncouth person. She obviously doesn't have a lot of morals if she takes you home the first night she meets you."

Once again, Jenni tried to sabotage any budding romantic interest for Chris, and it made Paul shake his head in reproach.

"You took me home our first date," Chris deadpanned.

"Chris! That is a lie and you know it!" Jenni screeched at him.

Paul and Chris laughed at Jenni's outrage.

"I'm kidding, simmer down." Chris tried to soothe Jenni.

Jenni rolled her eyes at them. "I came in here to ask if you know where I could get some paper and a pen?"

"Cassandra was using a pad and pen yesterday, and she put it in the drawer to the right of the sink. The sink is located in the room to the right of you called the kitchen. It's a place where people go to make meals. You should really try to get more familiar with it and maybe your man would come home for dinner more," Paul joked with Jenni, oblivious to the fact that Scott had been coming home late recently. Unknowing to Paul, it triggered a derisive reaction from Jenni.

"Maybe if *you* weren't so familiar with the kitchen, you wouldn't complain about the extra weight you have around your midsection." She abruptly turned and walked away.

Paul called after her. "You didn't hear me complain."

He turned to Chris, "What a bitch."

CHAPTER 17

S AM WALKED IN THE house through the back porch and saw the house was once again lively with activity as everyone was milling about making something to eat, talking, lounging on the furniture, or eating at the table.

I guess my solitude is over, she thought to herself as she took in the scene.

Sam walked in as the men were excitedly talking about their fishing trip and betting each other which one of them would catch the most fish.

Kari looked at Sam and commented, "Boys will be boys."

Sam laughed and playfully suggested, "Maybe you girls should make bets on who will find the best deal while shopping today."

"Oh my god, that actually sounds like fun," Megan mused.

Sam was surprised to see Megan was already up and about. She figured she would have slept to at least noon after last night.

"How was your walk?"

"So peaceful and placid. I'm surprised to see you up."

"I slept for a little bit, but once everyone was up, I could hear them all and it was hard to stay asleep. I will definitely be taking a nap this afternoon. Plus, the girls want to go to the outlets early, and I don't want to miss out on a shopping trip."

Megan looked over to Scott. "I left my lip balm in your car. Can I have your keys? I want to grab it before you go fishing."

"It should be open," Scott answered.

Megan motioned for Sam to walk with her to Scott's car since she was in conversation with her. "Do you want to go back to the outlets with us today?"

"I don't think so. I spent enough money the other day with Mia. I'll probably just stay here and lie by the pool, maybe go to the beach and read and act like I'm on vacation and not do much else."

"Sounds perfect."

"Oh, by the way, did you hear Joan Rivers is in a coma? Don't you watch her show?"

Samantha stopped dead in her tracks; it was silly but this news really affected her. She loved Joan Rivers and the practice of watching her show with her mother had become somewhat of a comfort and alleviation of bleakness in this period of her life.

"The Fashion Police has been kind of a ritual thing for my mom and me to watch together. That makes me so sad." Tears formed in Sam's eyes, but she didn't want Megan to see because she wouldn't understand what the ending of watching Joan signified to Sam. Sam thought she'd text her mom after everyone was gone.

"Yeah, I liked her too. Although she was old, she was relatively healthy. It goes to show you, you never know when your number is up."

"Life is very unpredictable and can change with the blink of an eye." Sam knew all too well how the fluctuation of life circumstances could mutate instantly.

As they walked out the front door, they noticed Jenni closing Scott's car door.

"I didn't see you slip outside," Megan commented to Jenni.

Jenni seemed a little daunted to see them but composed herself. "I was just looking for something I thought I left in the car, but I couldn't find it. Are you guys heading out somewhere?"

"No. I actually left my Chapstick in Sam's car and just wanted to grab it before we left to go shopping," Megan said as she walked toward Sam's car. "I think we're planning on leaving soon for the outlets. Do you need to take a shower and get ready?" She said this as a way to get rid of Jenni.

"Yes, I was just going to see Scott off and hop in the shower. I won't be long," Jenni said as she walked toward the entrance of the house.

Megan watched to see that Jenni was completely gone before she moved away from Sam's car toward Scott's car.

"What was that all about?"

"Jenni has been very jealous lately. I didn't want to give her any fuel for her suspicious mind by going into Scott's car while she was standing here. Plus I didn't want her to pepper me with details of last night. Did you know she sent Kari a text after y'all left to tell her to keep her eye on Scott? What is that horse crap? I've never seen her this insecure, and I don't want to be her next target."

As Megan was talking, she opened Scott's car door and noticed sunglasses and a folded-up piece of paper on the driver's seat with Scott's name scrawled across it. She moved the sunglasses to the dash, and she casually picked up the note from the seat and got in behind the steering wheel. Even though it was addressed to Scott, curiosity got the best of her, and she opened the note.

Samantha saw Megan open the paper and asked, "What is that?"

Megan scanned the letter. "I think Jenni really came out here to leave her husband a love letter. Isn't that sweet?" she said in a mordant tone. She folded the letter back up and opened the middle console to look for her Chapstick.

She reached in. "Here it is," and grabbed her Chapstick while dropping the letter inside. She shut the console and got out of the car.

"What did the note say?" Sam questioned Megan.

"Nothing too mushy, just something about meeting for a rendezvous."

"That's one way to keep the marriage interesting. I think it's great that she's trying to spice it up."

Megan responded to her, annoyed. "She could try to be a nicer person. That may work better."

"Do you really think she's that bad?"

Megan eyed her friend disbelievingly. "Have you not seen her behavior since we've been here? She's always so dismissive of people. I feel she has a haughty air when she talks to me."

"I actually experienced some of that contemptuous attitude last night. I asked her if she wanted to talk about anything that might be bothering her. She basically turned it around on me and made me feel worse about my situation."

"I warned you. I worked with Scott before he met Jenni, and I always thought the girl he married would be nice and friendly, like him. He is like the ideal guy—handsome, smart, funny, sweet, easy to work with, athletic, and kind."

"Sounds to me like someone may have a little crush on this guy."

Megan looked abashed. "Don't say that out loud."

They had walked into the foyer, and Megan scanned the area, making sure no one heard what Sam said, then she whispered, "That's all I need is for Jenni to think I'm after Scott. Yes, I hold him in high regard because I've worked with him, and I have a lot of respect for him. I need to get ready for the shopping trip." She turned to head up to her room.

Samantha shrugged to herself, not thinking it was as big a deal as Megan was making it out to be.

Samantha went to the kitchen to make a bowl of cereal. She could hear Kari and Justin conversing in the living room.

"You'll have tons of fun today fishing. You'd rather do that than stay with me and go shopping with all the girls, right?"

"I definitely don't want to go shopping, but I wish you and I could just hang out."

"Justin, we were basically by ourselves the first two days of this trip. Let's be a little social with the others. It will only be a couple of hours, then we'll have the rest of the day and night to be together."

"Do we have to go to that party tonight? We don't even know the host or any of his friends."

"Can we please go for a little bit? Then we can come home and snuggle." Kari kissed Justin and gave him a hug to reassure him.

Samantha appraised the exchange she had just heard. *Lord, Kari is constantly babying this guy. He sounds so co-dependent, and she portrays someone that is very independent. I can't see her putting up with him for the long haul, but who am I to judge what works for some people? I was discernably wrong about my predictions about my own relationship. Maybe she likes mothering him. It is sweet he wants to spend time with her but unappealing for him to whine about it,* Samantha thought to herself. *I'm better off alone than with a man like that, but he does seem to adore her.*

Paul was out on the porch filling a cooler with ice and beer for their fishing expedition. Cassandra had made bloody marys for the guys and herself and Misty, and they were outside, recalling events of the night.

"We all need the hair of the dog after last night," she said as she passed out the cocktails. Chris had grabbed his and went to take a quick shower.

"How many numbers did you collect last night, Cass?" Paul enquired as he ripped a bag of ice open to fill the bottom of the cooler.

Cassandra swirled her celery in her drink smugly. "Oh, a few."

"I think Jenni was nervous leaving her husband with you all night," Misty told her friend.

Cassandra scowled at that comment. "Jenni can be as nervous as she wants. I was busy with available men. But I may harass her and give her a complex about what happened or didn't happen last night, wouldn't that be funny?"

"She already has a complex, but yes, please take over my job and harass her while I'm fishing. I'll give you my scepter while I'm gone." Paul handed Cassandra a beer.

Cassandra eyed the beer. "This is your scepter?"

"Yes, it gives you power to be really sarcastic and funny. And once that one is gone, you just open another."

"Ha-ha, cheers to that," Cassandra said as the three of them clinked their classes.

CHAPTER 18

S COTT WAS IN HIS bedroom looking for his sunglasses. "Babe, do you know where my sunglasses are?"

Jenni looked thoughtful for a second. "Actually, Cassandra mentioned she accidentally grabbed your sunglasses last night when you drunkards got home. I guess she thought they were hers. She said she placed them on the driver's seat in your car," Jenni told her husband.

"Okay, good. We're taking Paul's car because I figured you'd want a car today. I'll grab them on my way out." He gave her a peck on the lips and headed out the bedroom door.

Jenni had searched Cassandra's room last night, looking for some indication that she and Scott were attached in some way, but she didn't find anything connecting the two of them. It wasn't like back in the day when people wrote notes to each other or carried pictures around. Every important message or photo would have been on her phone, and Cassandra had her phone with her. The only thing she found was a work appointment book where Cassandra had written meetings and lunch dates with clients throughout the book. There was not one entry with Scott's name indicating a meetup. Jenni felt foolish for even being so desperate to look in her room, especially since Sam had seen her coming out from there. But at this point in her life, she really didn't care what other people thought of her.

She had a mixed feeling of satisfaction and apprehension with how the formulation of her plan was being implementing in her mind, but that feeling was subsided by the morose feeling of realizing this could lead to the end of her marriage.

The sound of Cassandra's voice interrupted her thoughts as Jenni heard her call out to Scott, "Hey, good-looking, I made you a bloody. It's on the counter."

"Aww, aren't you a doll? I think that's just what the doctor ordered. We hit it hard last night, but it was totally worth it."

Jenni cringed when she heard this exchange. She knew that Cass talked that way with all the guys, so she lulled herself to dismiss the comments and focus on the task at hand. She knew if she just remained cool and collected and acted normal then she'd know for sure by the night's end if her husband was having an affair.

After everyone cleared out of the house, Samantha stretched out on the plush, overstuffed sectional in the media room and flipped through the channels to see what was on television. She stopped at the talk show, *The View*, and wondered how long it would take for all the hostesses to start talking over one another, where the viewers couldn't even distinguish what was being said. Recently, the media had uncovered that Rosie O'Donnell would be coming back to *The View*. Sam used to adore Rosie when she had her own talk show. She remembered watching it with her mom, Brenda, and always jokingly commenting how she wanted Rosie to be her best friend because she thought she was the kindest, funniest person ever. Then, when she became a host on *The View*, she seemed so angry and harsh. There was nothing more annoying to Samantha than a star who always spewed their political agendas in an intolerant, righteous fashion.

Just like Sam predicted, the antagonistic hostesses began their oppositions where you couldn't follow what was being argued, and Samantha slowly began to tune out. This made Sam think of her affinity for Joan Rivers. She texted her mom, wondering if she had heard the news. Brenda responded that she was also distraught and saddened by the news.

She wandered over to the majestic windows and plopped down in a chair that overlooked the beach. She knew she wouldn't have this constant overwhelming surge of melancholy forever, and sometimes she wondered if she was addicted to the sadness.

The sound of her text message tone alerting her was a welcome distraction from the dismal feeling. A smile crept over Sam's face as she began to read the text: "Hey, Sam, it's Jake. I got your # from Mia. I'll be in your area for lunch & I thought maybe I'll stop by and bring you something to eat. Let me know if you'll be around."

Mia must have told him I'd be at the house alone, Sam thought. *How considerate to think of me and want to bring me lunch.* She texted him back: "I'd love that. We can eat on the porch overlooking the beach. I'm not picky, so whatever you bring is fine."

Sam felt a little giddy about Jake coming over to see her, almost like she had regressed back to high school and she was the impressionable freshman cheerleader anxious for the cute senior football player to look at her and smile. Since her breakup with Brad, Sam hadn't felt any fondness for any other man, and she was beginning to think it would never happen again. It was comforting to know that Jake could be a welcome distraction from the never-ending upheaval of memories that cluttered Sam's thoughts.

She noticed it was eleven-thirty. She quickly grabbed her phone to text Jake, asking him what time he expected to be there. When he said he'd be there in forty-five minutes, Samantha sprinted up the stairs to take a shower and get ready. She had taken a long walk this morning, but she didn't want to smell like she did. She wanted to get ready and look good for him in that understated beachy-style hair down but a little disheveled, a touch of makeup with earth tones and bronzer to look natural.

The doorbell rang at quarter after twelve, and Samantha hurriedly threw on a cute beach cover-up over her bikini. She flew down the first part of the staircase then slowed her pace at the lower half, in case he was looking through the windowed front doors. She didn't want to appear too anxious. She could see him standing there in a short-sleeved button-down holding bags with the Wendy's emblem on them.

Sam opened one of the double doors and smiled brightly. "I didn't know the police department delivers." And there was that sexy grin, Sam thought as she ogled him.

"Only to super attractive females in distress."

"Distress? Who's in distress?" She led him to the kitchen.

"Well, I just figured that since there's a big party tonight, you'd be in distress on what to wear," Jake said with a laugh. "Isn't that usually how it goes with females?"

"Usually, but I'm not the typical female," Sam said as she grabbed two plates.

"I can attest to that!"

Sam grabbed a beer and poured Jake a glass of iced tea since he was on duty.

"I bought a burger and a chicken sandwich and some fries and a side salad, so you pick whichever you want and I'll eat the other."

That gesture resonated with her more than it would with other girls because it made her think how Brad never would have thought to buy options trying to please her. He would have bought two of the same things he wanted. She overlooked Brad's heedlessness because he didn't do things to be mean; he was just not thoughtful.

Interrupting her thoughts, Jake pulled a chocolate frosty out of the bag. "I bought you this for dessert."

"How did you get so thoughtful?" Sam asked hypothetically. She did think the concept would make an interesting study on how some men could be so chivalrous while others were so ignorant.

"I guess my mama taught me well."

And there you have it, Sam thought. Brad didn't have a relationship with his mother and had been raised by his narcissistic father who only thought of himself. Jake verified what Sam thought all along about Brad's inability to consider others.

"So how have you avoided the marriage trap so far?"

"Ha, interesting choice of words. I guess I could ask you the same thing." Sam hated that question because she knew most guys automatically judged a woman at a certain age that hadn't been married and was decent-looking as categorically crazy.

"I came close a couple of times. I thought my last girlfriend was the one, but she had other plans."

"I'm sorry you went through that. I experienced the same thing, and it's been tough." She took a long, hard pull of her beer and her chest tightened, disbelieving that Brad was actually gone and not the one. It still was hard for her to admit to herself, let alone other people. She set her beer bottle down, and they both stared at each other, wondering if they should delve into this conversation any further. They could see a touch of sorrow in each other's eyes and decided to change the subject.

Knowing they were going through the same thing took off some of the pressure of the expectations between them. Sam knew she wasn't ready for someone to replace Brad when she had so many unresolved feelings for him still. Plus, Jake lived over three hundred miles away—if she couldn't make it work with someone who lived twenty miles down the road, she sure as hell didn't want to test three hundred. Sam felt more relaxed with the insight of Jake's love life and their situation and feelings being parallel. The last thing she wanted to do was lead anyone on after wondering if her whole relationship had been a lie.

They spent the rest of their lunch reminiscing about high school stories, and Jake bestowed the gossip about mutual people they grew up with who still lived in town.

It was a nice, relaxing, friendly lunch, and when he had to go, Sam was already looking forward to seeing him later that night.

He looked at his watch. "Looks like I need to get back. Thanks so much for being my lunch companion today."

"Thank you for bringing lunch." Sam walked him to the front door.

"I'll probably be at Bubba's around eight-thirty. He tends to invite anyone he comes in contact with, so it should be an interesting assortment of people and it usually gets crowded."

"Cool. Sounds like fun. I'm not sure when we'll head over, but I'll see you there." She reached out to give him a hug, and as he drew her close, he kissed her cheek.

She closed the door and watched him pull away. That hour they were together, she felt like she had reverted to her twenties when there wasn't a care in the world and it was as if the whole purpose of living was to have fun. Those were the days—why did it have to get so difficult and complicated the older we get? she wondered to herself, shaking her head.

She was looking forward to tonight and maybe getting more than a peck on the cheek from Jake. A smile formed across her face thinking of the possibility. She plucked another beer from the fridge and picked up the *People* magazine from the counter and headed out to the pool.

CHAPTER 19

THE GIRLS DECIDED TO split up to go shopping. Kari and Jenni wanted to start their shopping at J. Crew while Misty, Cassandra and Megan were excited to check out the sale purses at the Coach store. They planned to meet back up at one-thirty to grab some lunch.

Jenni was slowly starting to drive Kari crazy with her incessant talk about Cassandra and quizzing her on what went on after she left the bar last night. Kari didn't understand the preoccupation of Jenni's interest in Cassandra.

"Do you think Cass is interested in Scott? Or maybe I should ask if Scott has commented on Cass and is it making you feel insecure?"

Indignantly, Jenni sneered, "Scott wouldn't comment on that floozy? I don't think I'm being insecure. I was just curious about the rest of the night, but I'm sure Cass wouldn't hesitate to pounce on my husband if I'm not around. What about you and Justin? I'm surprised he actually left you today to go fishing with the guys."

Kari was all too aware of the way Jenni would deflect topics she did not want to discuss further by being snarky about someone else's personal business.

"What exactly are you implying, Jenni?" Kari was trying to control her temper but she was getting sick of the snide comments Jenni kept making about her relationship with Justin.

"I'm just stating a fact, Kari. The boy doesn't seem to know what to do with himself if you're not there holding his hand. I'm not saying anything bad about you, but I feel like the longer you're with this guy, you'll start resenting him because you're always bending over backward to make sure he's comfortable in social situations. You're an outgoing person, but you have been holding back your social side to accommodate what Justin wants to do, which is usually nothing. I just think you could do better. He bores me."

Kari didn't feel like being combative and berate Jenni about her own relationship problems since Jenni had a truculent tenacity and would just come back and affront Kari's relationship more. Plus, Kari knew there was some truth in what Jenni was saying, but she wasn't wanting to discuss it further it this point.

"I guess I'm lucky that he loves me so much. I'd much rather be with a man that always wants to be with me than one who doesn't."

She left it at that and let Jenni draw her own conclusions by what she was implying, if anything, in that statement.

"Oh, look at the time. We need to go meet the girls for lunch." Kari was eager to change the subject and have a more stimulating conversation with the other girls than the negativity Jenni was spewing.

Megan, Cassandra, and Misty were having a good time brandishing different outfits for each other to mark their approval on. They all had a good laugh when Cass stepped out of the dressing room displaying a conservative cardigan pulled over a shirt buttoned all the way to the neck. She was wearing Audrey Hepburn *Breakfast at Tiffany's* sunglasses, and she swooped her hair in a severe bun. On the bottom half, her legs were exposed from the barely-there red-pleather booty shorts accented with clear Lucite stripper heels.

"What the… who are you supposed to be?" Misty wondered, staring at the incongruity of the outfit.

"This is my interpretation of Jenni. She puts on this prissy exterior, but we all know she must be a whore in the bedroom if she scored Scott."

They all collectively guffawed and consented to her explanation.

Cassandra and Jenni had a contentious relationship, and they both spoke acrimoniously behind each other's backs. Megan innocently asked Cassandra about the perceived rivalry between her and Jenni.

Cass told the girls that she had originally met Jenni when she found out the guy she was dating was also dating Jenni. Cass was in love with this guy, and it was devastating to her when she found out what a louse he was. Jenni had confronted Cass when she saw her with this man one night. When the guy spied Jenni, he tried to hide from her and told Cass he had to leave because he wasn't feeling well.

At first, Cass thought Jenni was cool, and she appreciated the awareness of what was conspiring behind both their backs. She thought that they could forge a friendship since this bonded them in an anomalous way. Cass tried to reach out to Jenni on numerous attempts to befriend her, and Jenni was receptive to a point. Cass finally realized that the only time Jenni truly contacted her was to find out if she was still talking to the guy they both had feelings for. Jenni would pry about the communication Cass still had with this man and would act as a sounding board for Cass to stay away from him. Cass really believed Jenni was trying to help her and look out for her welfare. Eventually, Cassandra drew the understanding that Jenni didn't really want to be her friend; she saw her as competition and an adversary.

Cassandra had felt betrayed by Jenni as a confidant and felt revulsion that she had played upon her heartache for her own benefit and not as someone who cared about their similar circumstance. They merged with the same crowd years later when Jenni started dating Scott and Cass was friends with his friends. She tolerated Jenni, but there was no love lost between the two of them.

The other three girls were all aglow, discussing the bargains they had purchased when Jenni and Kari joined them at the restaurant.

Megan greeted them by suggesting a drink special. "We just ordered the chocolate martinis. It's two for one right now! I love beach towns where they have great drink specials. Why doesn't Atlanta ever do that?"

"Some places probably do, but we're working while it's going on. Think about it, it's Friday and this deal runs from two till five o'clock. Most people are working during those hours," Kari reasoned.

"Ahhh, true. You're so smart," Megan kidded.

"A genius," Kari taunted back.

After glancing at the menu, Misty commented, "I wonder how the guys are doing and if we're going to be eating some fresh fish tonight."

"Is that what you're really wondering, or is someone thinking of a certain someone?" Cassandra playfully said to her friend.

"Yes, tell us what's going on between you and Paul. That's what we all really want to talk about—sex." Kari grinned at Misty.

Misty felt a little embarrassed that all the girls were staring at her, and she noticed Jenni rolling her eyes.

"He makes me laugh."

"Have you kissed him?" Kari pressed.

"Yes, but I'm not looking into anything. We're just having a good time."

"That's so sweet. I'm happy for you," Jenni told Misty condescendingly. Misty smiled at her weakly, knowing she was not being sincere and she knew she was just trying to cut off any further discussion about it.

"So, Cassandra, tell us about the guys you met last night." Jenni was obviously bored by the talk about Misty and Paul's budding romance and wanted to focus on what had gone down last night.

Cassandra glanced at Misty, feeling like Jenni had slighted her time to be excited and talk about her relationship progression with Paul, so she decided to antagonize Jenni a little.

"The men I met were all very sweet, but it was your husband who stole the show with his dance moves. I didn't know he could move like that. You know they say you can tell a lot about a man by the way he moves on the dance floor." Cass winked at Jenni when she said this.

Misty giggled, knowing Cass was trying to annoy Jenni. Jenni shot her a squinted glare.

"Oh, so you danced with Scott?" Jenni tried to sound as nonchalant as she could.

Although this would have been a perfect opportunity to make something up that happened between her and Scott to rile Jenni up, Cass didn't want to be totally knavery about the situation last night, "Actually, no, I didn't. He spent his time dancing with Kari and Megan."

"Yep, and he can move. We had a blast. I wish you would have stayed." Kari didn't think twice about telling her friend that her husband was a good dancer and she wasn't going to let Jenni's insecurities inhibit what she said.

Megan looked uncomfortable and kept quiet. She wasn't going to elaborate on Scott's dancing skills. She didn't feel the need to have Jenni cross-examine her actions.

Jenni smiled sweetly. "I was tired, or else I would have stayed. Scott definitely has all the right moves." She winked back at Cass. "I'm so glad you all had a great time."

Megan tried to change the conversation. "I'm going to take a nap when we get home since tonight should be off the chain. Sam said this guy throws epic parties. Jenni, I'm sure tonight will be a ton more fun than last night and you won't miss out," Megan reassured her.

"Oh, I'm really looking forward to tonight. We all will have so much fun together," Jenni said in an uncommonly mellifluous tone they weren't used to hearing from her.

She smiled at Cassandra, thinking to herself that hopefully tonight she would find out, one way or another, if there was anything going on between her and her husband.

Jenni addressed the group of girls with a jubilant façade. "I'm sure it will be epic in more ways than one."

CHAPTER 20

"SAM, COME UP AND see the stuff we bought," Megan called down to Samantha from the porch overlooking the pool. Walking up the stairs to the porch, the two French doors was open, and Sam could see a slew of shopping bags littered all over the floor. The girls were excitedly pulling out their merchandise for Sam and each other to admire. By the end of the fashion show, each girl had a pile of clothes covering the entire surface of the living room furniture.

The girls were complimenting each other's purchases when the guys walked in.

"What the heck happened here? Did you leave anything for the other shoppers?" Paul joked when he saw the piles of clothes.

"Honey, I can't wait to show you the deals I got," Jenni pulled Scott closer to her.

Scott looked around helplessly at the other guys, hankering for a way out.

Chris slapped him on the back. "We don't have wives, so we'll bring the fish up from the cooler. Have fun." He laughed and turned with Paul to make a quick exit.

"I'd love to see what you bought," Justin said to Kari as he grabbed her hand and kissed it.

"On that note, we'll go help Chris and Paul with the fish and see what you guys accomplished today." Cassandra led the three other girls out.

Scott stood there with a spurious smile on his face and a cata-tonic stare as Jenni showed him each piece of clothing she purchased. Justin, the complete antithesis of Scott, oohed and ahhed as Kari displayed her garments.

After the last item was exhibited, Scott gave Jenni a perfunctory compliment and quickly exited to join the others outside on the porch to discuss their fishing adventure.

Justin and Kari were going through her stuff, contemplating what she would wear that night. This made Jenni envious of the way Justin was so engaged and affectionate with Kari while her own husband couldn't have departed faster.

Jenni stood in the living room feeling alone, preoccupied with her thoughts. She looked at Justin and Kari and realized everyone else was outside on the porch. This was the perfect opportunity to implement her plan. She went to get the pad of paper and the pen she had put in her room.

In the privacy of her room, she scribbled the lines, "Leave the party and meet me back at the house around 11:45. I need some private time with you. —S." She folded the note and headed back to the living room.

Kari and Justin were absorbed in examining and discussing which outfit would be best for the party scene. Jenni feigned rearranging her clothes and discreetly picked Cassandra's receipt out of one of her shopping bags. She casually wrapped the receipt around the note and put it in her pocket. She went to the kitchen and returned the pad of paper to its original place.

Jenni joined the others on the porch, and Kari and Justin followed shortly after. Jenni was biding her time for the perfect opportunity to get Scott to deliver the note.

Paul was entertaining everyone with his ribald storytelling skills about a previous fishing expedition he had taken involving a couple of amply chested women, drunken fishermen, and a broken-down boat. Everyone was laughing by the end of his story, except Jenni, who was concentrating on her plan.

Paul announced he was going inside to wash his hands and grab some cold ones for himself and whoever wanted one.

Jenni took this opportunity to melodiously say, "Honey, can you go and make me a mixed drink?" She smiled sweetly at her husband.

He begrudgingly agreed and graciously asked if any of the other girls wanted a mixed drink. As everyone was focused on Scott taking orders for drinks, Jenni slyly took the note and receipt out of her pocket and hid it in the palm of her hand.

As Scott walked away from the group to go make the requested drinks, Jenni called out, "Oh, Scott, just a second."

She walked away from hearing distance from the group. "I totally forgot I had Cassandra's receipt. Since you're going inside, could you put it on her pile of clothes in the living room? It's right next to my clothes." She didn't wait for him to respond. "Thanks," she said, and she turned to join the group again.

Scott walked inside and stood dumbfounded at all the clothes in the living room. He was nebulous to which clothes pile was even Jenni's. While she was showing him her wares, he was daydreaming about the fish he pulled in.

Paul noticed Scott standing there staring bewilderedly at the different piles and he commented, "Isn't it ridiculous how much women love to shop and spend money."

Scott turned around and laughed, "Ridiculous."

He then just picked a clothes pile and put the receipt on top of it. He figured that if it wasn't the right pile, they would return it to Cassandra, and he joined Paul in the kitchen to make a couple of mojitos.

Scott looked up from making the mojitos as Megan, Misty, and Cassandra walked inside and announced they were going to lie down for a bit before dinner and get rested for the party tonight. Justin trailed them to the living room and dutifully collected Kari's things as the girls picked up their own stuff and took it to their rooms. Scott glanced at the last pile of clothes and was grateful the receipt wasn't on his wife's pile. He grinned thinking that at least he hadn't messed up and put the receipt on her pile or she would know he wasn't truly paying attention to her.

Scott and Paul walked back out to the porch and Scott handed his wife and Kari the cocktail they requested.

"It's not a date." Samantha told Chris.

"What's not a date?" Scott wanted to know.

"Sam has a date with that cop that was at AJ's last night." Chris told Scott and Paul.

"Ugh, Chris, you're so full of shit. His name is Jake, by the way, and I do not have a date with him tonight. He was invited to the party, and I happened to be going also. That's it."

"But he did bring her lunch today," Chris needled Sam.

"Are you going to let him feel you up?" Paul bawdily asked.

Jenni immediately remonstrated, "Really! Must you always be so lewd? You're repulsive."

"Relax—stop acting like you're such a prude. I'm trying to help the girl. She's dealing with a broken heart and could use a good tune in Tokyo session."

"I don't even know what you are talking about," Jenni said as she looked at Paul with antipathy.

"Ah, come on, Jenni," Scott chimed in, "you know that movie from the eighties where he tells the girl to put her hands on her head and beep and he uses her boobs as radio dials to tune in Tokyo?" Scott got up and demonstrated the stance with his hands on his head and started twisting and chanting, "Beep, beep, beep."

Kari jumped up to help with the parody. She stood in front of Scott and used his chest as dials while saying, "Tune in Tokyo."

Everyone started laughing except Jenni as she shook her head in bewilderment. "I guess I missed that one."

Justin walked out as everyone was laughing and Kari was in the middle of fondling Scott's chest.

"Hey, sweetie, whatcha doing?" Kari wondered as she hugged Scott after their skit.

"Nothing, I just came out to help with cooking the fish and getting it ready for dinner. I took your clothes to our room to help clean up."

"You are so thoughtful." She gave him a peck on the cheek.

"Now, that's the type of guy I need. It would never occur to most men to do that," Sam praised Justin.

"Scott,"—Jenni looked at her husband expectantly—"did you happen to take my clothes to our room since you were in there?"

Scott looked at her mutely, not sure how to answer as to not make her upset.

"Jenni, Scott is a normal guy—no offense, Justin. Didn't you hear the psychologist? It's not normal for most men to do those things." Chris offered Scott a reprieve.

"Plus Justin isn't married to Kari," Scott added, not helping his defense.

"What does that mean?" Jenni looked at her husband with confusion.

Samantha laughed, "So basically, if I want a man to do thoughtful things for me, then I should never marry him?"

"Well, I didn't mean that—I meant…"

Paul interrupted Scott, "Jen-needy, how's that drink you're sipping on?"

Jenni looked at him quizzically. "Fine."

"Who brought you that drink? Oh, that's right—it was Scott, who was thoughtful enough to get up and make you that drink, so shut your ass up."

"Exactly." Chris high-fived Paul.

Jenni frowned at both of them.

Scott quickly turned the conversation back to Sam and her cop friend before Jenni could browbeat him about Paul's comment. "Are you excited to see Jake tonight?"

"Actually, I am. I think it will be an interesting night."

CHAPTER 21

CHRIS INVITED MIA OVER for dinner, and as usual, she showed up late. After dinner, they were hanging on the porch having a cocktail while everyone else was inside getting ready for the party.

"Are a lot of your ex-boyfriend's friends going to be at this party?"

"Nah, he works for Bubba. He may know a lot of these people, but they're not his friends. Jake will be there, who is his friend, but I've known Jake since high school."

Samantha walked out to join them.

"You must have heard Jake's name and came running," Chris said when he saw Sam coming toward them.

She punched his arm playfully and took a seat at the table. "You better watch it, Chris. If you get out of hand tonight, I'll tell him to cuff you and take you in."

"Maybe if you get lucky, he'll use the cuffs on you."

"Nice. Now I understand why you and Paul are best friends. You have the same track minds."

"You know what they say about great minds..."

"They're lascivious and lecherous?"

"I don't know that first word you used, but yes on the lechery."

Samantha and Mia burst out laughing at his comment.

"I'm heading upstairs to change and do my make-up," Samantha said as she got up.

"Try to look lascivious," Chris joked. "Did I use that word right?"

"Depends. Let me know when you see me."

Cassandra was doing her hair while Misty was trying on different outfits. She modeled Cass the second outfit she put on.

"No, go with the first. You looked sexy in it. There may be some cute men at the party tonight. I think you should definitely be looking instead of hanging on Paul's hip. Plus, if Paul is really interested in you, he'll find it enticing to see you being desirable to other men. Believe me, men like to feel challenged."

"I'm not one to play games," Misty said in a petulant tone.

"I'm not asking you to play games. I'm asking you to have fun and keep your options open."

"No, I'm sorry. You're right. I've just been feeling a little insecure. I didn't want to mention this because it's embarrassing, but I heard Jenni talking to Paul about me, and she basically told him I was ugly and he could do better. It really hurt my feelings and made me want to rip her eyes out."

Cassandra stopped doing her hair and went to her friend to give her a hug. "Misty, do not pay that witch one bit of attention. She puts down others because she thinks it makes her look better. She knows that all she has going for her is her looks, and so she rips on everyone else. You are much more than that, and she probably feels threatened by you."

Misty didn't believe Jenni was threatened by her, but she appreciated and needed the reassurance from Cassandra.

"Thanks, Cass. I hate the way it makes me feel because I was teased all growing up. Kids called me ugly and a ghost. But as an adult, I feel better about myself. So when things like this happen, I didn't realize how easily it is to slip back to when I was ten years old and plotting to hurt the next kid that made fun of me."

"Oh, you better watch what you say. If you were a kid in this day and age and said that, you'd be expelled from school and searched for weapons in your book bag." Cass laughed at the thought of Misty really being a threat because she couldn't picture it.

Misty laughed too. "Yes, that's true. I wasn't too big of a menace. My plots consisted of a rope tied to two desks so the bullies would trip and be laughed at."

Cass snickered at her friend. "Remind me not to mess with you!"

Downstairs, Kari was modeling her new outfit for Justin. Justin was always very complimentary to Kari, but he also had a distrustful side that would come out a lot when they were going to be in a social situation.

"You look so beautiful. Are you dressing for me, or are you trying to impress someone else?"

"Justin, don't be ridiculous. I want you to be proud to be my boyfriend."

"You know I'm proud even if you were to wear sweats and a T-shirt. I just don't trust any drunken fools that may be there tonight. If it were up to me, I'd prefer to stay home and have you all to myself."

"Sweetie, we stay home all the time. We're on vacation. Can you please have a good time tonight and socialize with everyone?" Kari was beginning to feel like Justin's babysitter, and it was getting tiresome.

"Please don't make it sound like I'm a child." Justin's voice was raised with a choleric edge. "You act like I'm a social retard. I spent my whole damn day fishing with your friends. I thought this was a vacation for us, not for me to spend time with your friends. I'm sorry that I don't enjoy drinking all day long and then spending my night with more people that are just trying to get drunk." Justin felt hurt by Kari's rejection.

Kari turned around so Justin couldn't see her roll her eyes. She was used to his fiery outbursts and knew Justin was sensitive and got his feelings hurt easily, but she just wasn't up to catering to his emotional needs at the moment.

"Just because people enjoy a couple cocktails doesn't mean their sole mission is to get wasted. We're not in our twenties any more. But I really hope that you're ready to socialize because I'm going to have a good time regardless."

She didn't want to be mean, but she was looking forward to the party and he wasn't going to manipulate her into feeling guilty about going. She planned to have fun with or without him.

"Are you almost ready?" Scott impatiently asked his wife while she was fixing her make-up in the mirror.

"Scott, you don't have to wait for me. I'm sure the boys are already having a drink on the porch. Go ahead and join them."

Scott was astonished by Jenni's considerate suggestion and didn't wait around for her to change her mind.

Jenni had actually finished getting ready, but she wanted Scott out of the room so she could strategize the scenario she had in her head. She stood in the middle of the bedroom, looking around. They had one of the master suites in the house, and it was expansive. To the right of the main entrance into the suite was a sitting area that was adorned with a love couch and overstuffed chair. The couch was beige with coral-colored accent pillows. The chair was a combination of the colors in a striped pattern. A glass-topped coffee table was positioned in the middle with a stunning mounted piece of coral. The amalgamation created a cozy and relaxed beach vibe.

There were French doors leading out to a private balcony. Scott and Jenni kept these doors open whenever they were in the room, especially at night. They loved that they could hear the sound of the waves crashing onto the shore, lulling them to sleep.

Jenni heedfully took in the beauty and peacefulness of the room and the juxtaposition of what might occur later if Scott and Cassandra showed up and she was waiting for them.

She wished she could ignore her intuitive notion about Scott having an affair, but it was impossible to act oblivious to Scott's change in behavior. She reasoned with herself that if no one showed up, she'd let go of her perception of why Scott had been acting distant. She noticed the note that was put in his car was not there anymore and he didn't mention receiving it, so he obviously didn't think it was from his wife. As much as she hated to think about it, she knew something was going to happen tonight.

CHAPTER 22

SAMANTHA CHOSE HER FAVORITE emerald-green strapless beach dress that made her eyes shimmer with more intensity. She wore her dark, silky hair straight, and it hung below her bare shoulders. She accented the dress with a cluster of gold bracelets and a delicate gold chain adorned with a starfish around her neck that Brad had gotten her when they had gone to the beach one year.

"Every time you wear that color with gold bangles, I always think of Elizabeth Taylor in *Cleopatra*," Megan said as she scanned Samantha.

"And every time I wear this, you say the exact same thing."

Megan decided to wear heels tonight and was towering above Sam even though Sam was wearing four-inch strappy black stilettos.

"I love when you wear heels when we go out. I can always find you in a crowd."

"At least my height is good for something because it sure doesn't help me in the dating world. I swear it's like Mission Impossible finding a guy who is taller than me—and that's without heels!"

"Is your friend Mia coming over soon?"

"She's actually here. She came over and ate while you were showering and is downstairs having a cocktail with Chris."

"Ahh, so does she really like Chris?"

"She likes him for the time she'll spend with him. That sounds bad, but she isn't looking for something serious with someone who lives in Atlanta. She had a bad divorce and has two kids, so she likes to have fun when she can. Besides, she said that she thinks Chris still has feelings for Jenni. What's that all about?"

"Really? That's funny because I always forget they went out before she met Scott. Chris does seem to have this love-hate thing going for her, which is easy to do with her. Well, maybe not the love part." They both laughed.

"That's interesting Mia made that comment. What did he say to make her come to that conclusion?"

"She said that he mentioned taking Jenni out a couple of times and then she said he acted almost scorned about the whole situation. She said it was a little off-putting, but then she thought why should she care if he still holds a torch for her."

"Hmmm, that *is* interesting. Maybe that's why he hangs out with all of us so he can still be near her." Megan kidded about the situation.

In her best Lester Holt voice, Samantha recites, "A beautiful woman is stalked by a man who only wants to be near her, on the next episode of *Dateline*."

Megan and Samantha had an inside joke that all their dating scenarios could wind up being an episode on *Dateline*.

They passed Cassandra and Misty's room, and Megan knocked on their door to see if they were ready to head downstairs. Their faces looked a little grave as Megan opened the door and peered in the room.

"Is everything okay?"

Cassandra bounded up from the bed and put on a big smile. "We are good to go."

Cass felt bad that Misty was feeling unsure about herself because of Jenni's comments, but she didn't want it to ruin their night.

The girls complimented each other's appearance. Samantha thought Misty looked pretty all dolled up, but she now understood that it must be hard for her to be noticed when Cassandra was standing next to her. Cassandra was wearing a high-waisted white skirt with a white crop top, revealing a tan and toned flash of midriff. With that outfit and Cassandra's kittenish demeanor, she was bound to have plenty of guys vying for her attention tonight.

As the four women headed out to the porch to join the others, Chris and Paul started whistling and catcalling.

"Dang, I feel a heat wave from all that hotness!"

"Looking good, looking good… not you, me!" Paul taunted the ladies.

"You wish you could look as good as us, Paul," Cassandra mocked him.

"Ah, yes, I do wish I was as hot as you so then I too could be called a slut."

"Someone would have to actually want to sleep with you to be considered a slut, my darling."

"Touché. I love when you can be such a Cass-hole."

She clinked his glass. "I learned everything I know from the biggest asshole."

"So, Mia, what is this party going to be like tonight? Who's the host, and is he pretty cool?" Kari asked.

"The hosts name is Bubba Hilder, and my ex-boyfriend captains his yacht. That's how I know him. He's a great guy. Charmer. His parties are usually a lot of fun with plenty of alcohol and a vast array of people. He's never met a stranger."

Scott stood up. "Let's do this, people!"

CHAPTER 23

THERE WERE EXPENSIVE MODELS of cars lined up and down the street as the gang walked toward Bubba's beach house.

Chris eyed a Lamborghini and Jaguar as he passed them. "Are you sure we will fit in with these people?"

Mia smiled at Chris. "What do you mean? Isn't your Jag in the driveway at your house?"

"No, it's in my garage, next to the Bentley," Chris played along with her.

"It's not like anyone will ask for our tax records to get in the party," Scott remarked.

"Thank God I've got my looks. With these looks, I have access to anywhere I want to go," Paul said as he kiddingly smoothed out his eyebrows.

"Paul, with those looks, you couldn't get access to the bathroom," Jenni deadpanned.

"Oooohh, she got you there, brother," Chris harassed him.

Paul was getting infuriated with Jenni's antagonistic ways. He appreciated someone that could give shit back to him, but he knew Jenni had malicious intent with the things she said.

"Clever, Jenni, and you'd be waiting in the bathroom line with me if they judged on congeniality."

"Jeez, do you two ever get along? Locked in a room, one of you wouldn't come out alive," Kari eyed them both.

"Yeah, 'cause I'd kill myself if I was locked in a room with that numbskull." Jenni winced.

"Someone please lock us in a room together," Paul said hopefully.

Mia nudged Samantha. "That's Jake's car. You better have fun tonight and not think of what's-his-nuts."

"Well, now that you brought him up…"

"I didn't say his name, so don't even go there!"

"Okay, okay. No *B* word or thoughts of him. A couple more drinks and I won't even know his name."

"That's my girl!"

Mia walked into Bubba's house with the rest of the crew following behind. Inside, the house was filled with a copious amount of people. It looked like a scene from a trendy club in Miami where all the women were beautiful, scantily dressed, majorly enhanced, and really tan.

Bubba was walking past when he saw Mia enter, and he came to greet his guests. He was clad in tan linen drawstring pants and a white linen shirt unbuttoned just enough for a carefree appeal. As the consummate beach bum, he had on his flip-flops but still exuded the aura of wealth.

"Welcome. I'm so glad you all could come. There's a band outside by the pool, downstairs is what I like to call the sports bar area, and speaking of bars—there's one right here,"—he pointed to the bar in the main room—"downstairs, and outside. Please enjoy." He kissed Mia on the cheek and turned to greet other guests.

Mia was immediately approached by people she knew and became engrossed in conversation. Chris, Paul, and Scott wanted to check out the sports bar downstairs, and the rest followed except Samantha and Megan.

They strolled to the bar that was located in the main room of the house. Samantha didn't want to appear too eager to find Jake, so she opted to get a drink first.

They both got gin and tonics and made their way out to the porch to listen to the band playing below by the pool. They stood by the railing to look over and observed the people outside surrounding the pool. Sam scanned the crowd for Jake, while Megan leisurely browsed for any cute guys. Megan pointed out Cassandra and Misty talking to two guys below by the pool. Unfortunately for Misty, the two gentlemen seemed to fawn over Cassandra and looked like they were both captivated by her charm while ignoring Misty.

It made Sam reflect on how hard it was to meet someone you really connected with on all levels, and then thoughts of Brad flowed in the cataract way by always submerging all her cognitive processes. She shook her head to dissolve the ideation and desires and tried to focus on the reality of her life. She chastised herself for ruminating constantly about her past relationship. She reminded herself that there was a very handsome man somewhere at this party that would take her mind off her despondency. She decided this was a good time to go look for Jake. As she turned from the rail, she almost ran smack into him.

"Whoa there, darling, you in a hurry to get somewhere?" He smiled his lopsided smirk and Sam grinned back at him, as her doleful memories receded. She was pleased that her search was just made easy.

"I was just wondering where you were, perfect timing. You remember my friend Megan?"

"Of course, good to see you again. This is my friend and co-worker, Matt Young."

Matt was a behemoth of a man with bulging biceps and a short military crew cut. He definitely was not the cop you'd want confronting you if you were the cause of a dispute. Megan smiled coyly, and Sam knew she was happy to meet Matt.

"Finally, a guy I can actually look up to when he's talking to me," Megan said under her breath to Sam.

Matt asked Megan to join him in getting another cocktail, and she willingly obliged.

Jake and Sam found a quiet corner on the porch where they could sit and listen to the music and not be jostled in the crowd of people. They made small talk about the party, but Samantha wanted to delve into more personal matters even though she consciously knew it might bring her down.

"Do you still talk to your ex?"

Jake looked at her, a little surprised by the question, but answered, "Hell no."

"Really? Why not?"

"Well, first of all, she broke my heart and started dating another guy. Secondly, I don't want the pain of talking to her. Why? Do you still talk to your ex?"

"He won't talk to me. He says it's too hard to talk. It makes no sense to me that he doesn't want to be with me yet finds it too hard to talk to me. I always thought we'd be friends... well, hell, I thought we'd be married and together forever. So it blows my mind that this is the same person who now can't talk to me." Samantha knew that this subject probably wasn't the most appropriate discussion when you're interested in a guy, but she'd known Jake for years and wanted his opinion about the situation.

"Samantha, men don't like to deal with their emotions, and rather than confronting our feelings, we run and hide. You said you ended things because he wasn't ready to get married and he has past issues he needs to deal with. He may have never married you if he isn't right with himself, so it was almost inevitable that you'd break up. Sucks, I know, and I'm sure you hear this all the time, but it's truly his loss." He placed his hand over hers and leaned in and kissed her cheek.

Sam blushed. "I thought I was the psychologist."

"But you're human too. Now let's have some fun. Let's grab a drink and cut a rug!"

"Cut a rug? Are you my grandpa?"

"I'll be whatever you want me to be." With that wicked smile, he stood up and grabbed her hand to lead her downstairs where the band was playing.

CHAPTER 24

SAMANTHA LOOKED DOWN AT her watch and couldn't believe it was already one o'clock in the morning. The party was still in full swing, and she didn't feel the least bit tired. She and Jake had bumped into a couple of people they had gone to high school with that Mia and her ex had introduced Bubba to. She spent most the night catching up with them and finding amusement in all the rehashed stories from high school. It was the first time that Sam had an enjoyable time without thinking that she wished Brad was with her.

Paul walked by and nudged her. "We're heading back to the house... going to night swim in the pool. Bring coppy-poo."

"You already look like you've been swimming." Sam looked at Paul standing there in his swim trunks.

"Yeah, I had to get on my swim suit when I saw the massive hot tub."

"You were intrigued by the massive hot tub or the massive boobs *in* the hot tub?"

"Don't judge me," he said with a straight face but was kidding with her, "or in your case, don't analyze me."

"You're too cute. I'll be back to the house shortly, and I'll see if 'coppy-poo' wants to come." She told him and made quotation marks with her fingers for the nickname Paul had given Jake.

"Cute, huh? Well, if he decides not to come, I'm available for any pleasure you're looking for."

114

Samantha laughed out loud. "You're so thoughtful."

"I aim to please."

She took him by the shoulders and turned him around. "Aim that way. You'll have more luck."

"So you're saying there's a chance," he called over his shoulder as he headed out the exit to the beach.

Jake walked up to Sam. "What was that all about?"

"He said they are going swimming back at the house and told me to have you come over."

"It's after one in the morning and they want to keep it going like an after party? I feel like I'm in my twenties again."

Samantha felt a little dejected. "So you're ready to go home?"

"Hell no. Who wouldn't want to feel like they're twenty again?"

She was happy he had decided to come back to the house.

Samantha took off her heels, and she and Jake headed down to the beach to go the back way to the house. They both recapped how the night had gone and agreed it had been an enthralling time. Samantha was in the middle of telling him about a favorite song the band sang and who was dancing when Jake stopped walking. She looked back at him quizzically. He grabbed her by her elbow and pulled her into his chest. He wrapped his arm around her waist and took his hand and grabbed her jaw. He forcefully kissed her mouth while moving his hand to the back of her head and tilting her mouth up by pulling her hair a little. Her head felt dizzy from a mixture of alcohol, passion, and desire. This was not love but lust and precisely what she needed at this point in her life. She reciprocated his domineering approach and grabbed the back of his head. She hungrily put as much force back in her kiss. Simultaneously, both of his hands descended her back, and with every movement, he used his hands to press her body harder against his own. Desirously, both his hands seized her butt and drove her pelvis into his. She groaned eagerly and kissed him deeper.

Although she was totally engrossed with kissing him, she thought she heard her name being called faintly. Then she heard the yell of Jake's name and she pulled back from him. She turned in the direction of the call and saw a shadow of a person running toward them. At this time of night, the only light on the beach was from Bubba's house lights, so Samantha couldn't make out who was approaching them.

The person called out her name again, and Sam responded, "Yes?"

"Come quickly, we need Jake."

Jake and Samantha started jogging to meet the voice calling their names. When they were able to distinguish who was asking for them, they saw it was Cassandra.

"Oh my god, there's been an accident," she said with alarm. She didn't waste time in turning her gait back to where she came from for them to follow her.

"What happened? Who's hurt?" Jake caught up to Cassandra and immediately got into police mode.

"It's Jenni. We think she fell and she isn't responding," Cass panted.

Cassandra led them to Jenni's bedroom, where Scott was kneeling over Jenni's body.

"Does she have a pulse?" Jake asked while he quickly made his way over to where Jenni was lying.

"We don't think she does," Chris answered for Scott, who seemed to be in shock, cradling her torso.

Jake firmly laid his fingers on Jenni's trachea to feel for her carotid pulse. He felt a faint pulse yet there was no movement of her stomach. He asked Scott to move to the side so he could perform CPR.

"What happened?" Samantha asked whoever would answer.

"We're assuming she fell. She has a wound on her forehead like she had tripped and fallen and knocked her head on the coffee table. Scott found her lying there."

In between doing CPR breathing and chest compressions, Jake turned to the others. "We need to clear this room and allow the paramedics and police to get in."

Paul and Chris grabbed Scott and walked him out of the room. Samantha had already started looking around the room to make sure nothing was patently askew. She walked over to where Jenni was lying and noted a small amount of blood on the carpet.

The paramedics arrived and immediately went to work on trying to resuscitate Jenni. They placed an oxygen mask over her nose and mouth and put her on a stretcher to race her to the nearest emergency room.

"What are you thinking?" Jake looked at the scrutinizing expression on Sam's face.

While Jake was performing CPR, Sam took note of the scene and noticed Jenni had changed out of her outfit into her pajamas. She was wearing a tank top with drawstring pajama pants. The one thing that caught her eye was that both pant legs were pulled up. Immediately her mind went back to the conversation she had had with her father about the pajama pants she bought him and how he had complained that they rode up during the night when he was under the blankets. Is it possible they would stay up if Jenni got out of bed and walked across the room? If she really hit her head on the coffee table, her pant legs should be down. Or did someone lift her out of bed and place her on the floor?

Sam pointed out the pant-leg dilemma to Jake and voiced her suspicion.

"Is there motive for anyone to want her dead?" Jake questioned Sam.

Samantha answered earnestly, "Unfortunately, if the last week of living in this house was videotaped, everyone would be a suspect... including myself."

CHAPTER 25

JAKE WAS BUSY GIVING orders to the other professionals that had showed up to the 911 call. He introduced Samantha as a clinical psychologist who was going to help him on this case and listed her credentials with the Atlanta police force. She was surprised of his appointment but was more than willing to help out. Jake was obviously revered at his job, and they all obediently listened as he took charge of the situation. He directed Samantha to get a statement from everyone in the house and to ask if they'd be around for further questioning if needed.

Samantha walked out to the main area of the house where the occupants of the house were gathered. Scott had been outside on the phone with his in-laws relaying the horrible news before he rushed out the front door to go to the hospital. Mia approached Sam after the bedroom was cordoned off and the police deputies were heading out the door.

"Hey, do you need me for anything? I kind of want to get out of here. I really don't know these people, and I feel a little intrusive being here."

"Yeah, it's a devastating circumstance. You were basically with Jake and I all night, but when you hooked back up with Chris, what happened when you came back here?"

"Not much. Paul got in the pool since he already had his suit on, and he convinced everyone else to get on their swimsuit. I was left outside with Paul because I was waiting for you to come back to see if I could borrow one of your suits. Then the tiny blond ran out of the house saying there'd been an accident and asked me where you and Jake were. I told her that y'all should be walking this way. She ran out to the beach, and I heard her calling your and Jake's name. Paul and I went inside to see what the commotion was about and never expected someone to be lying there like they were dead. That's basically it."

"She's not dead... yet. There's a chance she could survive."

"That's good to hear. I didn't particularly like the girl, but I didn't want to see her dead."

"Yeah, I hear ya. I have a feeling that may be the consensus. Okay, go home and get some sleep. If I need anything else from you, I'll let you know."

Samantha addressed the group of people she'd been living with for the past four days solemnly. She tried to give them a glimmer of hope since there was a faint pulse found. She relayed that Jenni was taken to the ICU and wouldn't be allowed visitors until she was stable. She explained she'd need a statement from each of them but it would be quick so that everyone could try to get some sleep, and she would pick up on specifics once everyone had gotten some rest.

Once Jake and Sam spoke to the last member of the household and everyone went to bed, they discussed some of the logistics of the tragedy. Everyone confirmed that Jenni must have left earlier and no one had realized it except Kari, but she thought Jenni was coming back. When they all got back to the house and Jenni wasn't with them, they figured she was in bed. Scott went to the bedroom to get on his swim trunks and see if Jenni was in bed when he discovered her lying on the floor.

Sam and Jake went back into the bedroom, and Sam role-played as if she were seeking Jenni. She entered the room and turned on the light switch on the wall. No lights turned on. She looked at Jake curiously. He watched as she walked to the nearest light and tried to turn it on from the knob on the lamp neck, and it still didn't turn on. She peered over the shade, and on further inspection of the lamp, she discovered the bulb was missing from the thread socket. She opened the drawer of the side table the lamp was placed upon, and there in the drawer was the missing lightbulb. She held up the lightbulb for Jake to see.

She noticed the lamp by the bed where the covers were pulled down was lit. Sam walked to the other nightstand to examine the other bedside lamp and found no bulb in it. She opened the nightstand drawer, and there was the bulb. A horripilation passed over her body. She had a feeling that this tied into what happened to Jenni tonight.

She raised the second lightbulb so Jake could see.

Jake responded, "Interesting."

She faced Jake with the lightbulb in her hand. "This was obviously planned."

"But why?" Jake questioned Samantha.

"Well, you'd think it would have been done by whoever was lying in bed. Since that was the only lamp in the room with a bulb, they could control what could or couldn't be seen when someone came into the room."

"From the way it looks, that person would have been Jenni."

"Yes, unless someone was waiting for her in the bed."

"That's a compelling thought."

"Yet I don't know if I buy it. I'm still convinced it was Jenni in the bed because of her pant legs being up. Besides, she was in her pajamas. She wouldn't have been able to change if someone was waiting in the bed to confront her. So we need to figure out who she was waiting for and who showed up."

"You had told me that you just met most of the people staying in this house. Do you have any insight on the dynamics of the relationships she had with these people? I figure you probably observed things from living with them this past week. What about her husband?"

"She was closest to Kari, although she wasn't particularly nice to Kari's boyfriend, Justin. She seemed jealous of Cassandra and accused her of flirting with her husband the first night. She was really insecure about her relationship with her husband. At least it seemed that way to me. I didn't notice any major fights where he came across as violent or doing anything to really warrant her insecurity. Well, besides the first night, when she accused Cass of flirting with him and he grabbed her by the arm to lead her away. It didn't look excessively aggressive, but who knows what really happens behind closed doors? The only thing I can say is he's a social guy who would dance with the other girls in the house when we were out, but I didn't see anything wildly inappropriate that made me question things.

"A different angle would be Chris's relationship with Jenni. He supposedly went on a few dates with her before she met Scott. Mia thought there might be some interest still there on his part from things Chris has said about her. It could be an obsession thing, but I'm only speculating.

"She and Paul had a somewhat volatile relationship. He liked to pick at her, and she didn't find it amusing. Misty wasn't a fan either, but I don't think it would have motivated her to do anything drastic. But who knows? People kill for less."

"Yes, they do. You wouldn't believe some of the absurd reasons I've heard for domestic violence and killings. It sounds like everyone potentially could have a motive to want to hurt her. I'm going to head out, but I'll be back tomorrow if you could make sure everyone is present for questioning." He wanted to hug her goodbye but thought the situation didn't warrant affection at this time.

After Jake left, Samantha made her way to her bedroom, wondering what was going through the other guests' minds. She doubted anyone was sleeping soundly. Megan was sitting on her bed when Sam entered the room, obviously waiting on her.

"Oh god, Sam, I can't believe this happened. I'm in shock. What are we going to do? Poor Scott... poor Jenni. You don't think I would have done this, right? I mean, I talked about her being a bitch, but I hope you don't think I did this. Do you?" Megan's eyes were as round as saucers, staring at Samantha, waiting to hear her reject the probability of Megan's guilt.

"Megan, calm down. I never said anyone is guilty, and I don't even know if there's a person to blame. Get some rest, and hopefully there will be more answers tomorrow." Sam turned out the light to prevent further discussions on the matter. She did find it odd that Megan would automatically assume she'd be prosecuted for what happened. Was there something Megan was hiding?

CHAPTER 26

S AMANTHA TRIED TO GET up before the rest of the household roused to make sure no one decided to leave early. She knew no one would attempt to drive back to Atlanta after discovering Jenni hurt with a life-threatening situation, plus it was late and everyone had been drinking all night.

She put on a pot of coffee and waited for the house to wake up. She phoned her business partner to fill her in on the details of her vacation.

"Hey, Bridget, how's it going? I hope I'm not calling too early."

"Hi, Sam, it's good to hear from you. Honey, I have two small children. We don't ever get to sleep in anymore."

"How was the practice this past week?"

"It's just the same old story there—depression, anxiety, narcissism, self-esteem issues—regular day at the office. Tell me something exciting and hopeful."

"I don't know if this constitutes as the excitement you are wanting to hear, but one of the girls that came on the trip was put on life support early this morning."

"Life what?"

"She could die, B!"

"What!" Bridget was dumbfounded. "What do you mean? What happened?"

"We're not totally sure yet. It looks like she fell and hit her head on the sharp corner of the coffee table in her bedroom. We all had been at a party and drinking a lot, which might have contributed to the fall. I've been assigned to help the Okaloosa Police Department investigate, so I wanted to call you to let you know what's up."

"What?" Bridget couldn't get past the information she was just subjected to. "How did you get assigned to do that? Sam, is this a joke? I told you to go down there to find a man and get laid, but instead you might be dealing with a dead person? Only you, Sam. Only you."

After she hung up with Bridget, she made a call to her parents. As soon as Sam said there'd been a horrible incident, Brenda put her on speaker phone so Dan could also hear what Sam was saying. She disclosed the magnitude of the current situation about one of the houseguests and clarified to them that foul play wasn't a certainty. They wouldn't know anything conclusive until they received notice that she died and they performed an autopsy or if she recovered and was able to say what happened.

Her father was intrigued with that kind of stuff and wanted to hear all the details. She bargained with him that when she got home, if he had a martini with three olives waiting on her, then they would go through the minutiae of this case. He readily agreed, and she knew a Manhattan would accompany him in that discussion.

She explained how she had seen an old high school friend who was a police investigator out at AJ's and then saw him at the same party and that's how she inevitably got involved in helping out with the investigation. She made it seem like a causal acquaintance so they wouldn't ask any other questions about Jake.

Her mother voiced her concerns about Samantha staying in a house where there may be a murderer. She reassured her mother that if someone did hurt Jenni, she seriously doubted they would attempt to harm anyone else when there were police lurking around everywhere. She reiterated that the tragedy may have just been a bizarre accident and that's why they hired her to go over everything and talk to the other guests in the house—to make sure there were no loose ends.

Once everyone got up, they were milling around the house, wondering if they should be at the hospital waiting to hear about

Jenni's condition or wait where they were until further notice. There was an uneasy sense of foreboding looming in the stillness of the air. The palpable reality of someone almost dying in the other room made everyone laconic and withdrawn.

Scott was not with the others. He had left the house after notifying Jenni's parents of the unpleasant circumstances and followed the ambulance in route to the hospital. Chris and Paul had decided to drive to the hospital after Scott to offer support, but Scott convinced them there was nothing they could do and he'd rather be alone. He assured them he'd keep them informed and persuaded them to go back to the house to get some sleep.

He had texted Samantha what number he could be reached at, and she was planning on going to the hospital after talking to the rest of the household first.

Everyone had questions for Samantha.

"Do we have to stay in this house for any purpose?" Cassandra asked precariously.

It was a haunting feeling for everyone, knowing Jenni was lying in one of these rooms with the life draining out of her.

"Why are we being questioned if Jenni got hurt from an accidental fall?" Paul wanted to know.

"What is the police saying about the situation?" Megan asked Samantha.

"This is dreadful. I don't know how long I can stand to be in this house," Kari tearfully announced.

Samantha put up her hands to stop the questions and speak to all of them at once.

"Everything that has occurred is routine in any incident that involves someone in critical care. We have to cover everything, even if she did get hurt as a result from an accidental fall. Jake will be over shortly, and we ask that we can speak to each of you individually for more in-depth questioning."

Samantha was bombarded with questions again.

"Who gets to go first?"

"What are the rest of us supposed to do while waiting to talk to you?"

"Can we leave and come back?"

Samantha knew this was hard for all of them and empathized with the impact of knowing Jenni could die.

"Let's just do this alphabetically. So, Cassandra, you'll be first. Meet us in the library at eleven-thirty. I'd prefer if everyone stayed near the house, but you're free to go swimming or take a walk on the beach, but just be cognizant of when it's about to be your turn. Remember, this is just a routine interview, so there's no need to be worried about what you should or should not say."

Just then the doorbell chimed, and Sam told the group, "That should be Jake now. We'll be in the library." She looked at Cass. "We'll see you in fifteen minutes."

Samantha went to let Jake in. He was wearing khakis with a golf shirt. His expression was somber until he looked her up and down, and then that infamous grin appeared.

"You look adorable."

"Jake, really? Isn't your mind on other things?"

"Darling, I do this for a living. I'm good at multitasking."

Samantha had her dark hair tied up in a messy knot on the top of her head. She had only put on tinted moisturizer and swiped mascara on her lashes to look somewhat presentable. She was tired and didn't feel particularly adorable, but she had to admit the same thought had gone through her head about him when she opened the door, but she didn't think it was appropriate to be flirty under these circumstances.

Jake followed her to the library as Sam spoke about the others' concerns about staying in the house. She informed him they all agreed to stick around to answer any questions and Cassandra would join them in fifteen minutes to go over what she recalled.

The cavernous study was adorned in rich dark leather, from the books to the furniture, giving it a regal Victorian feel opposed to the rest of the house's lambency. Jake took a seat in one of the high wing back chairs feeling a little out of place compared to the sturdy metal chairs from the precinct he's used to.

He looked at Sam earnestly and said in a hushed tone, "I'm glad they've all agreed to stick around since we can't hold them here by law. I would imagine that if there is a perpetrator amongst them, it would look suspicious if one of them refused to talk to us or left early without knowing what truly happened to Jenni last night."

"I haven't noticed anyone acting suspicious. They're all concerned and perturbed over what has happened, which is to be expected. Hopefully, these interviews will detect something awry that will clue us in to what really occurred last night."

"That's where your expertise comes in handy, my dear. I figured you'd be able to detect bullshit faster than the average bear. Also, I'd imagine you'd be more competent to analyze their statements and be able to come up with shit I didn't even think of."

"Ah, come on, Jake, you don't give yourself enough credit. I'd think dealing with bullshit would be your biggest forte."

"Are you implying I'm full of shit?"

"I'll just say you're rehearsed on the subject."

"That may be true, darling, but only a woman can hear a statement and get a whole other meaning from what one is saying." He gave her a wink and a grin.

"You're lucky you're cute or else I'd think that statement could be a tad sexist."

"Thank God I have that going for me or I'd have lawsuits coming out my ass."

"I won't sue you as long as I get special privileges."

"You got it!"

"You didn't ask what special privileges I wanted."

"Oh, I assumed that was a double entendre for wanting to sleep with me."

"Jake!" She slapped his arm playfully. "That is not what I meant, and why would that be a special privilege?"

"Sleep with me and find out." *There's that seductive smile*, she thought to herself.

"Okay, okay, we have serious work to do. Can we please focus?"

"You can try."

CHAPTER 27

CASSANDRA KNOCKED SOFTLY ON the door to the library. She slowly entered the room, uncertain what to expect.

"Hey, Cassandra," Samantha said in an upbeat tone and smiled warmly at her to make her feel more at ease. "You can take a seat on the sofa. We're going to go over some stuff with you and ask you about the previous day's activities."

She nodded and smiled with pursed lips.

"Let's start on the night you came back from AJ's. What time did you guys come home, and was Jenni awake?"

"We got home around two. No, I didn't see Jenni. I assumed she was sleeping in her room."

"Who was still up, and what did you guys do?"

"It was Scott, Megan, Kari, and I that drove home together. You guys had already left, and Chris went home with Mia when we left the bar. When we got back here, Misty and Paul were still up hanging out and we joined them for a drink. Paul, Scott, Kari, and Megan got in the pool. Misty and I headed for bed shortly after, and Paul said he was tired too and was getting out of the pool. That's all that happened that night."

"Did Scott check on his wife at all?"

"I guess so. He went in his bedroom and changed into his swim trunks. He did make a comment to Megan and Kari that Jenni was sound asleep."

"So you and Misty went up to bed and Paul went to his room while Megan, Kari, and Scott stayed in the pool?"

"I went to my room alone. Misty and Paul were talking and I was tired. I don't know when they decided to head to bed."

"Meaning Misty didn't sleep in your room?"

"Right. Since Chris was out for the night with your friend, Misty decided to sleep in Paul's room."

"Okay. The next morning—walk me through—did you notice anything unusual?"

"Unusual? No. I did hear Jenni nagging Scott about what time he finally came to bed. I heard him say he fell asleep on the couch and that's why it wasn't until early that morning that he finally got into bed. She didn't seem too happy with the situation."

"Did they have this discussion in front of everyone?"

"No, I was walking down the hall, and their bedroom door was open. I overheard."

"Was there anything else that was said?"

Cassandra looked at Sam hesitantly.

Sam probed, "Are you not wanting to tell us something?"

"Scott's my friend, and I don't want to make anyone look like a schmuck."

"Look, Cassandra, I don't know Scott well, but it was obvious that there were a few problems in their marriage. Hell, I don't know anyone who can say they don't have problems in their relationship. It's normal to have disagreements with your spouse. Now what did Scott say?"

"It's not what Scott said—it was Jenni who was upset about things and mentioned how he had been coming home late from work a lot lately. She asked him if he was having an affair. He said she was being ridiculous and insecure."

"Was that it?"

"Yes. I kept walking after that because I didn't want one of them to come out and know I heard them."

"Before I got back from my walk on the beach, what was everyone discussing?" Samantha questioned Cass, not really knowing if it was relevant, but she wanted to make sure she covered all the bases.

"Scott had come down from his room to eat breakfast, but Jenni didn't come down then. He went outside on the porch to eat cereal, and Kari went out there and joined him. Justin had taken a shower and got dressed, and I told him Kari was outside. He glanced out there but surprisingly didn't join her. He ate his breakfast inside at the breakfast bar. He asked how our night went and said he was glad he went home and got his sleep since he had a good ride that morning. Megan came down and made breakfast, and I asked her what time she made it to bed. She said she went up shortly after I did. Scott and Kari came back inside, and the guys started to discuss their fishing trip and that's when you came back from your walk."

Cassandra walked Samantha and Jake through her shopping trip and admitted to provoking Jenni about Scott's dance moves but said it was harmless fun.

Samantha asked her about Misty being upset over Jenni's comments she made about her to Paul.

"How did you know about that?"

"Misty was talking about it the night we got home from AJ's. She seemed pretty mad at Jenni and was very hurt by the whole conversation."

"Yes, Misty told me while we were getting ready for the party. It pissed me off too. Jenni is... umm," Cassandra paused, feeling bad for saying negative comments about someone who could possibly die. "She can be so insensitive, and she attacked me the first night for being friendly to Scott. I don't want her husband, and I don't appreciate the constant slight of the eye from her and the judgement about my single lifestyle."

"What do you mean she judged your single lifestyle?" Jake wondered out loud.

"Oh, just the fact that I'm single and go out on a lot of dates. In our twenties, Jenni and I dated the same guy. We had this contention between us because of it. After she got married, I let it go since I knew we wouldn't be pursuing the same guy anymore, but she never seemed to get over it."

"I see. So last night, when Misty told you what she overheard Jenni saying to Paul, it made you mad at Jenni again and maybe fueled feelings of your past rivalry with her?"

"Yeah, it did. She can be imperious about a lot of things. She has a superior attitude about being married and having someone. Her belittling us single girls is maddening."

Samantha nodded. "I understand. Being single is hard, and she kind of did the same thing to me about my breakup. She wasn't very sympathetic."

Sam tried the concept of relatability to Cassandra's experience to make Cassandra feel comfortable expressing her true feelings about Jenni.

"Ha, the queen of cold, but I try not to let her get under my skin."

"It seemed she got under Misty's skin. I didn't think she had it in her to be as acrid as she was about Jenni." Sam tried to lead Cassandra on.

"It takes a lot to work Misty up, so I knew Jenni really must have really hurt her. Misty is usually an extremely laid-back person, but you don't want to do her wrong because she doesn't forgive or forget easily."

"Tell me about the party and who you were with and what you were doing before you came and got Jake and me after finding Jenni in her bedroom."

"When we got to the party, I went downstairs with the crew to check out Bubba's sports bar area. The guys put their names down to be the next for the pool table and we all got a drink at the bar. Since they were waiting to play, I asked Misty if she wanted to walk outside to see what was going on out there. It was really crowded. We met two really nice guys right off the bat. We stood there and talked to them for a while. Then Mark—that was the name of the guy I was talking to—asked me to dance, and we left Misty talking to his friend."

"Do you remember where you were around eleven-fifteen? Who did you see from the house?"

"Gosh, let me think. I was dancing with Mark a lot of the time. I did excuse myself to go find the others, probably around eleven or a little after. I went inside but didn't see any of the guys playing pool. I went upstairs to check it out and was approached by a really handsome guy. He kind of cornered me, and at first I didn't mind, but he tended to drone on and on about himself. I finally saw Misty walk by, and I grabbed her to get away from boring dude."

"Do you know what time that was?"

"I do. I looked at my phone because I wasn't interested in what that guy was saying and it was quarter till twelve. That's when Misty walked by."

"Do you remember the guy's name you were talking to?"

"Umm, I can't remember." Cassandra squinted her eyes and wrinkled her forehead trying to recall. "I'm bad when it comes to names, and like I said, at first I was interested in talking to him, but the longer we spoke, the more I realized the conversation was all about him and how great he is—it was a total turn-off. I think he said he was in real estate, and maybe that's how he knows Bubba?"

Samantha wrote that down in case she needed to check up on Cassandra's alibi, but she didn't want Cassandra to think this man may be essential in the avowal of her whereabouts during the time Jenni was presumed to have been hurt.

"What happened next?"

"I grabbed Misty and told her to follow me to the bar so I could get clear away from that guy. She seemed a little upset, and I asked her if everything was okay. She told me that while I was dancing she had liquid courage and wanted to find Paul to hang out with him. She said she saw him talking to some really beautiful women and she felt too embarrassed to go up to him because she felt inferior to those women. Then she watched him excuse himself and he walked out of the party to the beach access. She decided she would follow him since he was alone and she could talk to him in private and maybe get some smooches. He was heading for the house, and she followed him there. When she got inside the house, she didn't see him. She figured he must have been in his room changing. She said it dawned on her that this may look stalker-ish if he came out and saw her just standing in the living room waiting on him, so she left. I guess that's when I saw her, but you'll have to ask her that."

"Okay, then did you get a drink?"

"Yes, we actually did a shot. We both needed it. I told her that Paul is just a social guy and not to fret too much about it and we should go look for him and the others. Megan happened to walk by and she joined us in a Jager shot. I asked her where the others were, and she said she hadn't seen anyone in a while."

Jake stopped her to ask, "Did Megan say where she'd been?"

"Not really. She commented that she needed a shot too, and under her breath, she said something about being irritated. I figured she met some guy and I asked her about it and told her of the lame guy I had just wasted time talking to. She said that her situation was something like that. Eventually, we made it downstairs and saw Scott throwing darts with some random guy. Megan stayed to watch Scott throw. Misty and I walked outside, and there was Paul in the hot tub with some girls, and Chris was close by, talking to a girl. Kari and Justin were sitting on a couch listening to the band, and I think Chris said you both were over by the bar outside somewhere. Misty and I hung out with Chris and Paul, and then Paul suggested we take the party back to our pool since no one else had their bathing suits on. We took the beach access back to the house, and when Scott went to change into his suit, he discovered Jenni on the floor of their bedroom. I knew y'all were on your way back here. That's when I ran up the beach to get Jake."

Jake and Sam both nodded, waiting if Cassandra had anything else to add. She was finished with her summary, and Sam ended the interview. "Thanks, Cassandra, can you tell Chris to come in here please?"

After Cassandra walked out of the library, Jake commented, "So what do you think of everything she said?"

"I'm waiting to make any assessments until I hear what everyone else says, but it's never good when you can't remember the person's name you were with when a crime may have been committed."

CHAPTER 28

C HRIS WALKED IN THE study, and it was obvious that he was physically rattled by Jenni's condition. He had dark circles looming under his beady eyes, and his face was drawn and pale from a lack of sleep. It was understandable that Chris would be upset with Jenni's critical state, considering he had been interested in her at one time and may still have some lingering desires.

"Chris, I'm sorry about this tragedy. I know you had a past with Jenni and you went out on a couple of dates with her before she was married," Sam sincerely addressed Chris.

Chris was a little taken aback that Samantha knew about him dating Jenni but then recalled that he did tell Mia and figured this is how Sam found out about it.

"I'm very saddened by the unfortunate event. Jenni could be a pain in the ass, but I always found her beauty beyond compare. She had an aura to her that was very mesmerizing," Chris said this looking straight ahead, almost like he saw Jenni standing there, and with a faraway expression on his face, he smiled.

Although Samantha thought Chris's words were a tad on the creepy side, she agreed, "Yes, Jenni was quite pretty. What happened between you two that it didn't work out?"

Chris seemed to snap out of his trance and looked at Sam and Jake like it was the first time he noticed they were in the room.

"Oh, it just wasn't meant to be between us." His words sounded like an actor reciting a line he didn't believe in.

"Scott was perfect for her. He's everything a girl would want in a man. I could never compete with Scott. Jenni and I remained friends, and then Scott and I became friends. It all worked out the way it was supposed to… well, until last night."

"Let's talk about last night." Jake wanted to steer the conversation away from the overly saccharine commentary of Chris's relationship with Jenni and Scott.

"You guys went fishing that morning. Did anything unusual occur before you left?"

"Not that I can remember. I had stayed the night with Mia, and she dropped me off at the house in the morning. I thought everyone would be waiting on me, but Paul was the only one up. He told me Justin had just finished a bike ride and was in the shower. Paul was eating breakfast, and I was going to join him when Jenni appeared out of nowhere. She harassed Paul and me about hooking up with Misty and Mia—almost like she was jealous. I guess she was originally looking for some paper and a pen and asked if we knew where she could find some. Paul told her she could find it in the kitchen, then he gave her a hard time about not knowing how to cook, and it escalated to Jenni snapping back about Paul being fat. Typical Jenni," Chris said, shaking his head, "if she feels degraded, she'll come back harder. Then the rest of the household woke up, and we went fishing."

"Did her comment about Paul's weight make him mad?"

"Of course it did. Paul has zero tolerance for Jenni, and she pushes his buttons like no other."

"Did Paul ever talk about hurting Jenni?" Scott got to the point.

Chris immediately realized he might have led Sam and Jake to believe that Paul wanted to harm Jenni. He shook his head to deny any kind of violence. "Paul wouldn't touch a woman no matter how mad she made him. I just can't see that happening, nope."

Samantha had expected that response from Chris. She has interviewed friends of people accused in violent and homicidal cases and most had unequivocally denied that their friend could be capable of such acts.

Samantha switched the conversation back to Jenni searching for a pen and paper.

"What did Jenni need to write down?"

"I have no idea, she didn't say. She seemed preoccupied and not in the greatest of moods. Paul and I definitely didn't want to engage her further."

Sam wondered if Jenni wanted the paper for the note that Megan found left in her husband's car asking for a rendezvous.

"Was anything said about Jenni or the other girls while fishing?"

"Hmm, I'm sure. Let's see,"—Chris looked up and pursed his lips—"we joked to Scott about Jenni being a pain in the ass, and he admitted that she'd gotten bad about the nagging and it was starting to weigh on him. That was the extent of that conversation. You know how guys are—we don't go too deep. When we got back to the house, Scott had to sit through Jenni's fashion show while Cass and Misty helped Paul and I get the fish out of the truck. They were bashing Jenni,"—Chris's voice quivered—"and I just laughed along. The girls were complaining about dealing with her at lunch. They commented that they wished Jenni would have gone fishing with us and joked about throwing her overboard if she was on the boat. If hindsight was 20/20, we would never have been joking about that."

"Of course not," Samantha reassured him.

Jake cut to the chase. "At the party, where were you between eleven and twelve?"

"I was with Paul most of the night, talking to some girls. He was talking to these two girls who got in the hot tub, so of course, Paul wanted to join them. He ran to get his bathing suit at the house. The girls got in the tub, and I didn't want to be the sleazy guy standing there trying to talk to the girls who were half-naked at the party. I excused myself, and I went to look for Mia. Mia happened to be outside also and was standing with you guys. I asked if she wanted to go upstairs with me to grab some food. She said she was in the middle of telling a story but would meet me in a bit. I walked up the porch stairs while Megan was coming down them. We stopped and talked and she said Justin was up there by the rail all alone and I should join him. She asked if I knew where Scott was, and I told her no, and she said she was going to go look for you." He looked at Samantha.

"I pointed at where you guys were standing and told her I'd see her after I grabbed some food. I roamed along the railing looking for Justin, but I never saw him—I guess he had just left that spot or maybe he found Kari. I went to the bar, got another drink, and then got some food and stood looking over the railing, listening to the band. I could see you guys below, but I guess Megan found someone else because I didn't see her with y'all. I noticed Mia was still deep in conversation, so I just chilled and ate and enjoyed the people watching. Then I stood in line for the bathroom for ten minutes, and by the time I came back downstairs and outside, Paul was already in the hot tub cutting up with the girls. Eventually, Misty and Cassandra came out and joined us, and they said Scott was inside throwing darts with Megan. Around one o'clock, we gathered everyone and headed back to the house to swim and hang out. Mia came too. When we got to the house, Paul jumped in the pool. Mia said she'd wait for you to see if she could borrow one of your suits. I walked past Scott and Jenni's room, and I heard Scott say, 'Holy shit.' I looked inside his room and saw him kneeling next to Jenni. I yelled to get help, and Jake and you showed up a couple minutes later."

"Did you see anyone else while you were eating and listening to music?"

"No, but while I was waiting to use the bathroom, I did see Justin from a distance. He looked like he was frantically searching for someone—which we all know was probably Kari he was looking for."

CHAPTER 29

NEXT ON THE LIST to talk to Samantha and Jake was Justin. Sam confessed to Jake she hadn't tried to really get to know Justin much this past week, but in her defense, she hadn't tried to go exceptionally deep with any of the guests staying in the house. She had been preoccupied with her own thoughts, and she hadn't looked at this trip as a bonding experience to have lifelong friends. She just wanted the solace of the beach and getting out of town. Besides, Justin was an introvert and reticent in most conversations and Sam wasn't there to extract life histories and long-term goals from these people. In retrospect, it would have come in handy now.

Justin moved like a cat, swiftly and quietly but innocuously. He sat on the couch and stared at Sam and Jake with an attentive and alert expression and seemed poised to receive a command. Sam attributed his demeanor to his many years training in the military. Sam had briefed Jake on Justin's accomplishment of getting into the Green Beret training class which was scheduled to begin in a couple of weeks. Jake and Samantha had a fondness for military personnel since they had grown up very close to Eglin Air Force Base. Jake's father worked as a civilian at the base for many years. Sam's own family wasn't directly associated with the military, but having grown up in a predominantly military town, she knew lots of families who were affiliated. Sam had reverence for people who fought for our freedom and had even dated a couple of Air Force Academy grads. It was impossible to live in Fort Walton Beach and not know someone interconnected with the military.

"How well did you know Jenni?" Jake questioned Justin.

"Kari and Jenni are pretty good friends, and because of this, I have been around Jenni and Scott several times since Kari and I started dating."

"How long have you and Kari been dating?"

"We've been together almost five months, but it seems like we've known each other much longer because we've been inseparable since our first date."

"Would you consider yourself good friends with Scott and Jenni?"

"I wouldn't say good friends. We have hung out as couples a handful of times, but I don't spend time with Scott without Kari."

"What was your relationship like with Jenni?"

"It was a friendly relationship, I guess. I think she was a little resentful of the time I took away from her friendship with Kari. Jenni and I don't converse a lot. We don't have a lot in common. She tends to be on the gregarious side, and I'm a lot more reserved. Kari enjoys her company. That's the only reason we were friendly toward each other—besides that, we were like night and day."

Sam thought to herself that Justin was using the word *friendly* a little leniently. Jenni never seemed very amicable toward Justin, but then most wouldn't describe her as having a genial character.

"Kari is pretty gregarious also," Sam said, hoping Justin would elaborate why he and Jenni didn't click as well.

"Yes, that's true. But Kari has the kindest heart I've ever experienced with someone. She is truly genuine and caring, whereas someone else may be gregarious yet it's because they want attention."

Sam nodded in agreement with his statement and knew he was referring to Jenni's conduct.

"Walk us through your night at the party."

"When we got there, we went downstairs and put our names down for the pool table. Everyone was hanging at the bar and having drinks, but I don't drink. I got a water. We waited until the people in front of us were done playing pool, and I racked the balls. We probably played for an hour. After, Chris and Paul started talking to some girls and Scott went to the bar. I went to go look for Kari. She and Jenni had gone outside while we were playing pool. I couldn't find her outside so I searched upstairs. I was a little frustrated, considering that wasn't really my scene, and she knew I would have rather stayed home with her. I scanned the crowd from the upper deck and caught a glimpse of her walking out to the beach with Scott, and I presumed Jenni was in front of them, but I didn't actually see Jenni. I figured they were going back to the house for something and would be back soon because I know Kari wouldn't just leave me. I went back downstairs and watched other people play pool and throw darts. I probably watched for ten to fifteen minutes then went outside and found Kari."

"What time was that at?"

"I'd say around eleven-thirty."

"Then what did you do?"

"We sat and listened to the band play and then left with the crowd. You know the rest."

"What did you do when you got home?"

"I headed straight for bed. I was ready to leave the party a long time before Kari was ready. I just wanted to go to sleep when we got back. Kari said she was really tired too, and we headed to our room. Then I heard Chris yell for help, and I got up and saw everyone in Scott's room. I guess Jenni drank too much and fell and it knocked her out, correct?"

"Possibly—since she's in critical care, we can't determine what caused the trauma to the head."

"Can we leave after talking with you guys? I'm ready to get back."

"We can't make you stay, but I would imagine Kari may want to stay to make sure Jenni survives. This is a very crucial time. She has swelling on her brain, and that's never good."

"Yes, of course, whatever Kari wants."

Justin stood and shook both their hands, and with very erect posture, he walked out of the room.

"He definitely is a military man. I thought he was going to shout, 'Sir, yes, sir!' at one point in the questioning. He must be a tough guy to have been accepted to the Green Beret training, but he struck me as being slightly possessive or clingy with his girlfriend, almost spineless."

"Yep, I got the same impression of him during the week, and Jenni didn't hesitate to chastise Kari about Justin being her shadow. I did overhear him whine to Kari about being away from her for too long. He's very protective and a little on the controlling side. He's nice enough and dotes on Kari but almost to the point you wonder if he has any other friends."

"It's a wonder he let her out of his sights for that long."

Sam laughed and nodded in agreement.

CHAPTER 30

THE NEXT NAME ALPHABETICALLY was Kari. It was a convenient circumstance that they would hear Kari replay her whereabouts right after hearing her boyfriend retell his night.

Samantha really liked Kari from the moment she had met her at the pregathering in Atlanta. Although Kari had some terse words with Jenni, Sam knew this would be hard for her since she was the closest friend Jenni had here.

Kari immediately started defending all of Jenni's actions throughout the week. It was obvious that Kari felt bad for having disagreements about the way Jenni disregarded Justin.

"Maybe Jenni was right the whole time about me and Justin not being a match. I got upset with her on several occasions when likely, she was just trying to have my back and she could see what was best for me."

Being condescending and rude was a strange way to show loyalty, but Samantha kept this thought of Jenni's rebuked words about Justin to herself. She knew Kari was feeling guilty about quarreling with her friend now that Jenni's life was hanging in the balance.

"Did Jenni not like Justin just because she didn't think y'all were a good match, or was there something more to it?"

"I don't think so. She found Justin to be boring and uninteresting. I think she was a little jealous of all the attention he lavished on me. Personally, I think she wanted Scott to be more doting and involved with her as Justin is to me."

"What did Justin say about the way she treated him?"

"He didn't care for Jenni, but Justin doesn't like many people. I mean, he does, but he's not one to be buddy-buddy with a lot of people. You know what I mean? He's an introvert and doesn't like a lot of drama and nonsense, as he would put it."

"What do you see in him? He does come across as a nice yet elusive guy. You seem like a more socially amicable person," Jake wondered.

"Yeah, we're opposites in that aspect, but Justin treats me like a queen. He does a lot of nice things for me and is very attentive. It was refreshing to have a guy actually adore you instead of all the pricks in Atlanta that dick girls around."

Samantha could relate to that statement, and she could see why Justin's treatment would be appealing to Kari, or any girl for that matter.

"You said it '*was*' refreshing. Are you really having doubts about your relationship with Justin?"

"I was. I talked to Jenni and Scott about it last night. I wanted Scott's opinion…"

"Hold up—let's start from the beginning, and we'll get to everything that happened last night," Jake interrupted her.

"You were the closest to Jenni. Tell us insight to what was going on this week with her and everyone else in the house, including her husband. There seemed to be some dissonance," Sam probed.

"Okay, who do you want to start with?"

"Let's start with Paul."

"Jenni and Paul have always had a volatile relationship. He's harmless. He's a big kidder and has this sarcastic wit that can be insulting to some, but he's just going for a laugh. Though you know what they say, many a true word is said in jest. I think Jenni took a lot of what he said personally since there usually is a tidbit of truth behind his remarks. He thinks Jenni is way too self-important, and he feels the need to bring her down a notch or two. There is no love lost between the two of them.

"Chris, on the other hand, still seems to carry a torch for Jenni. Jenni and I would talk about it, and she knew she still had some pull over him. I didn't agree when she would flirt with him to get him to do stuff for her like get her a drink from the bar or whatever. When she went out with Chris, she did like spending time with him, but she said she wasn't physically attracted to him. You see who she married, so that makes sense. Scott is definitely not hard on the eyes. I think Chris has accepted his role as just a friend to Jenni because he's also friends with Scott and he respects him."

"Did Scott notice or care that Chris still had feelings for Jenni?"

"Have you seen Scott? I don't think Chris could intimidate him. I doubt Scott gave it much thought. Jenni had tried to make Scott jealous by vying for Chris's attention, but it never worked. Scott is the epitome of the stereotypical good-looking, popular jock who never had to work too hard to get the best-looking girl. He probably never had to worry about other guys taking his woman. He just focused on his sports. "

"What was Jenni's relationship like with Cassandra and Misty?"

"Jenni and Cassandra's relationship is kinda tricky. They're more like frenemies. You know, friends and enemies. They had prior competitiveness with men when Jenni was single. I think they dated the same guy at one point. Strangely, Jenni has been acting paranoid about Cass's interactions with Scott lately. I don't know what brought on this jealousy because I haven't noticed a change in the way Cass and Scott interact with each other. I confronted her about it while we were shopping the other day, and she denied that she had any inclination that anything was going on between Scott and Cass. I didn't believe her, but I knew if I persisted she would get angry at me and I wasn't in the mood.

"As far as Misty goes, Jenni never tried real hard to befriend her. Jenni tends to act like an elitist, and if she thinks someone isn't up to par with her standards, then she doesn't bother with them. I hate that aspect of her personality. It is her loss because we all know that Misty is a terrific person."

"Were there problems in her marriage?"

"There definitely seemed to be tension between the two of them recently. Though Scott or Jenni never confided in me if they were unhappy with each other, so it's just my opinion. Yet, Jenni seemed overly concerned and protective of Scott, and he seemed a little annoyed by the treatment. But who doesn't have issues in a relationship?"

"Thanks for the overall view of her relationships. Now tell us about last night."

"As you know, all the girls went shopping, and I was excited to wear my new outfit last night. Justin thought my outfit was too sexy, and he was pouting about me wearing it and then about going to the party. He actually got heated about it and started an argument. Frankly, I had had enough of babying him. I had always felt bad about him not being comfortable around others so I would sacrifice not doing things to make him happy. It was wearing on me. That's when the concept of my relationship started getting tarnished and me having doubts about the longevity. The only reason I'm telling you this is because it pertains to the rest of my night.

"At the party, Justin knew I was being a little standoffish and agreed to play pool with the rest of the guys. Once they start playing, Jenni and I walked outside to mingle. I confided in her that Justin was smothering me, and I thought I would get the 'I told you so' speech, but instead, she just nodded. I asked if everything was okay, and she said she had a migraine. I knew it was eleven o'clock because she kept glancing at her watch. I asked her what time it was and if she was waiting for something. She told me no and that her migraine was making her fidgety. Then she suggested we go upstairs and take a shot to see if it would help her head. We did, and some guys approached us and started a conversation with us, but Jenni kept looking around and seemed anxious. She grabbed me aside and told me she was going to go back to the house to get some medicine. She emphatically told me not to tell Scott that she had gone to the house. She said she didn't want him to worry and come looking for her when she would be coming right back. She told me to tell him she was in the bathroom if I happened to see him and he asked. She encouraged me to keep talking to those guys, and she left." Kari got choked up after the last sentence, thinking that was the last time she had seen Jenni unhurt.

"I then did a terrible thing. I saw Justin come into the living room looking around for me. I slinked down between the two guys Jenni and I had been talking to, and they blocked Justin's view of me. I know... it was mean. I was having doubts, and I didn't want him around until I cleared my mind." She paused, looking sad, but continued.

"When I saw him turn toward the kitchen, I ran to the stairs and went to look for anyone else. I saw Scott in the game room and asked him if I could talk to him privately. I wanted his opinion on how I should handle my situation. I asked him if we could go somewhere where Justin wouldn't find us. He led me to the beach. Scott was so nice and made me feel better about the situation. He graciously told me that any man would be lucky to have me, and although Justin was a nice guy there would be someone else I may have more in common with. He said I should just enjoy the rest of my trip and deal with Justin when we got back to Atlanta."

"Did Scott ask where his wife was?"

"Oh, yes, he did. I told him that she was using the restroom because that's what she asked me to say."

"How long were you two on the beach?"

"Maybe fifteen to twenty minutes. While we were sitting on the beach, Paul ran by us and yelled he was going to get his suit on and we should too. We laughed and said maybe later. Then a few minutes later, Misty walked by and told us she was going to grab her cell phone at the house. Scott and I thought it was too coincidental that Misty was heading back to the house the same time as Paul without them planning a hookup of some sorts. We talked about that for a bit, and we both thought it was great they were having fun. Then we headed back to the party. We were on the boardwalk entrance to Bubba's backyard when I saw Megan walking toward us. She started chatting with Scott—about what, I don't know. I wasn't paying attention because I was scanning the party below.

"We were a little elevated, being on the boardwalk, and it made it easier to look through the crowd. I was looking for Justin. I saw him coming out of the house, and I knew I needed to stop avoiding him. I decided I wasn't going to deal with my issue that night, but it wasn't nice to just leave him alone at a party he didn't even want to be at. I caught up with him through the crowd, and he acted upset and frantic. He's not the sociable type, so I wasn't surprise he was amiss since I left him to fend for himself. I felt really bad I did that to him. We sat and listened to the band, and people watched and Justin seemed to relax."

"Was he upset with you?"

"Surprisingly, no, he was just happy to see me. He didn't comment on where I'd been, and I wasn't going to bring it up."

"How long were you at the beach when Paul ran by? Did you see him or Misty return?"

"We were probably out there ten minutes when Paul bolted by. No, I didn't see him or Misty come back, but we weren't out on the beach that much longer. I did notice Paul in the hot tub shortly after, so he obviously came back.

"We all left around one, and everyone was talking about going night swimming. Justin and I were tired and wanted to go to sleep. We went straight to our room, and that's when we heard someone yell and we went to look what happened." She shook her head in disgust, and tears formed in her eyes.

"I feel horrible that I was too caught up in my own problems that I didn't even think about Jenni. I just figured she went to bed. In fact, when we were all leaving, Scott said he couldn't find Jenni, and I said I thought she had gone home to bed. I feel really guilty about that."

CHAPTER 31

MEGAN WAS SAMANTHA'S CLOSEST friend in the house. She had known her for several years, and they both used each other as sounding boards and confidants. They'd shared frustrations with work, family, friends, and men throughout the years. They both knew they could count on each other for a morale lift or just an ear to bend. This past year, Sam had really relied on Megan's abutment of support in dealing with the Brad heartbreak. She was the one person who consistently reassured Samantha that everyone grieved on their own timeframe and that one day the pain would lessen, but until then, it was okay to take as much time as she needed to get over her loss. Sam felt somewhat normal when discussing Brad with Megan. She didn't judge Sam's inability to move past Brad and reassured her it would happen. She made Sam feel vindicated in her reactions and feelings she still held for a man that everyone else thought was unworthy of her time, since he couldn't commit to her wholly.

As Megan came into the room and took a seat in front of Jake and Samantha, she seemed nervous and fidgety. She was clenching and unclenching her fist and then began to wring her hands. Sam found this behavior a little peculiar for Megan, considering she knew Sam so well and shouldn't be apprehensive about talking to her and Jake. Yet considering the circumstance, most people would be jittery too, Sam thought to herself. Plus, Sam knew that although Megan was like a buoy when helping others in crisis situations, she herself was not as durable in her own life experiences.

"Hey, girl, are you doing okay?" Sam asked her friend with heartfelt concern.

"I'm kind of in shock. What happened, do you guys know something?"

"Not really. We're trying to put the pieces together, and that's why we're talking with everyone to make sure there was no foul play. Did you notice anything at the party like Jenni talking with anyone, leaving with anyone, anything suspicious?"

"I was with you at the beginning of the night, and then I met your friend…" She nodded at Jake because his friend's name escaped her at the moment.

"Yes, Matt." He helped her out.

"Right, Matt. Sorry, I'm horrible with names, and there's been a lot going on, obviously. I did see Jenni walking through the living room to the main entrance. I didn't think too much about it or really wonder where she was going. I hate to say it, but I didn't care if she was leaving or not at the time. Am I a horrible person to say that?" She started clenching her fists again.

"Meg, you're just being honest with how you felt, so no, I don't think it's horrible. You had no way of knowing what would happen," Sam reassured her.

"Do you know what time you saw Jenni going out the front door?"

"I'm not totally sure. I would say around eleven. I'm not positive."

"Were you with Matt all night, Megan?" Jake wanted to know.

"We hung out for a while, and he's a really nice guy, but he knew a lot of people that were there, so I started to feel like a hindrance. I didn't want to make him feel like he had to entertain me. I told him I was going to go look for you, Sam.

"Oh, and I did notice Justin standing on the porch overlooking the party shortly after I saw Jenni leave. I was going to go up to him and ask where Kari was, but I didn't want to get stuck talking with him in case he didn't know where she was. He's not really Mr.

Excitement. Geez, I'm coming off as a bitch, aren't I?" she said with a nervous laugh.

"You're lucky I know you because you kind of are," Sam said with a knowing smile, kidding her friend.

"On my way down the porch stairs, I saw Chris. He said he was going up for some food, and I asked if he'd seen you, and he said he hadn't. I told him Justin was up top by the corner railing and he should go say hi. He said he would. I tried to find you guys, but I must have overlooked you. I eventually saw Kari and Scott on the boardwalk coming from the beach, so I went to hang with them. Scott and I spoke, and Kari went to find Justin."

"Did Scott ask you where Jenni was?"

"Not that I recall."

"Did you see Paul come back to the party with his suit on?"

"I don't remember seeing him return, but I did see him in the hot tub later."

"Did you move from the boardwalk with Scott?"

"Oh, that's right. I did ask Scott if he'd walk down to the gulf with me since it was dark and you never know who could be looming in the shadows. I wanted to feel how warm the water was and get away from the chaos of the party. That's probably why I didn't see Paul come back."

"Did you happen to walk back to the house for any reason or did Scott?"

"No," she said with wide eyes. "The thought that we were so close and could have helped her is daunting. I mean, I guess we could have helped. I'm not totally sure what happened."

"That's what we're trying to figure out."

"How long were you out on the beach with Scott, and what kinds of things were you discussing?"

"Not long. I came back to the party probably five or ten minutes later. Scott and I just talked about the trip and fishing, nothing too in depth or memorable. When I walked back in the party, Paul was in the hot tub, and Chris was over there also. I went upstairs to find Matt. Instead, I saw Cassandra and Misty about to take a shot at the bar, so I joined them."

"Cassandra mentioned you were irritated about something and said you needed a drink."

Megan looked at her searchingly and squinted her eyes. "I don't recall if I was. If I was irritated, it was probably due to it being very crowded in there and someone bumped into me and got their drink on my outfit."

"I see. Where was Scott?"

"Scott? Oh, he stayed out on the beach. I told him I was heading back to the party, and he said he was going to take a couple minutes of peace and quiet before he would return. He mustn't have stayed out there too long since he was playing darts when Cass, Misty, and I came downstairs. They went outside and hung out with Paul and Chris, and I stayed and watched Scott throw darts.

"We all decided to leave around one. When we got back to the house, I went up to our room to change into my bathing suit when I heard yelling. At first I just thought they were being rowdy and having fun. I came out of our room and saw everyone standing down the hall by Jenni and Scott's room. It's so sad. I can't imagine what Scott is going through right now."

"Did it not cross your mind that Scott was supposed to meet Jenni back at the house according to that note we saw in his car? What did the note specifically say?"

"I totally forgot about that note. I can't remember verbatim, but it said something along the lines of 'I miss not being able to touch you all week, let's meet at eleven-thirty tonight back at the house while everyone is at the party. No one will even notice we're gone.' She stopped and realized how that may make Scott look bad and said, "I doubt he even saw the note because I put it in his middle console."

Samantha wondered if Megan knew that her last comment made her look suspicious.

"Have you talked to him since?"

"No. I sent him a text asking if I could do anything for him. I haven't heard back."

Once Megan left the room, Jake turned to Samantha. "Did you know what the note said?

"Not literally. Meg told me it asked about meeting up later. She didn't read it to me."

"Do you not think it's strange that it said they haven't been able to touch all week? If his wife wrote that, why wouldn't they have been able to touch all week if they were sleeping in the same bed?"

"Yes, that registered as odd. We need to ask Scott to see that note... maybe Megan was mistaken by the wording."

"I know she's your closest friend here, but there were a couple of inconsistencies in what we were told and what she said. Nothing huge. She knowing about the note is another story."

Sam caught the disparity in some of the occurrences Megan told them, but she also knew her not to prevaricate about things. "You're referring to Chris telling us he pointed out where we were standing to Meg when they met on the stairs. While she just told us Chris didn't know where we were when she asked. Plus Cassandra said Megan implied she was irritated with a guy with whom she was talking to. Yet she told us she was irritated by someone bumping into her. Yes, I noticed, but she may have forgotten that Chris told her where we were. She was drinking a lot. Cassandra also said that Megan didn't say it was specifically a guy hitting on her that was irritating her. Cassandra said she told Megan about the guy who kept talking about himself, and Megan said her irritancy was similar. She could have not wanted to go into it with Cass because it was insignificant. That's not really inconsistent, but I did note it.

"I was with Megan when we saw the note left in Scott's car. Yes, I can see that looks bad, but she pointedly told us she saw Jenni leave the party. Would she have told us that if she left shortly after and hit her over the head with something?"

Jake stared at Samantha seriously.

"What?" Samantha asked disconcertedly.

Jake hesitated but then said, "You're not being biased, are you?"

Offended by his question, Samantha scowled at Jake. "Of course not. I'm even going to quiz you about the procession of your night because I don't presume anything and I know anything is possible."

The devilish grin appeared. "Atta girl."

CHAPTER 32

MISTY WAS DREADING HER interview with Samantha and Jake. She knew she'd have to reveal that she followed Paul to the house last night and, like a child, she had run when faced with the reality of how creepy that might have appeared to him. Now she had to confess this embarrassing detail to people she didn't know well. Her stomach tightened when she thought about it. If this disclosure wasn't bad enough, she now looked suspicious due to the fact that she didn't have an alibi during the time Jenni may have gotten hurt. Although she didn't know Samantha well, she had expressed ill will toward Jenni recently. All these thoughts were racing through Misty's mind as she was sitting across from Sam and Jake, waiting for them to start their questioning of her night.

"First of all, I want to tell you that I never wanted Jenni to get hurt even though I know I said some things that may have indicated otherwise," Misty blurted out when Samantha looked up at her to begin.

Sam was thrown a little off guard with Misty's comment and wondered if she was guilty of anything. "We all say things we don't mean, Misty. Did you know Jenni was hurt when you went back to the house?"

"Gosh, no. I didn't really see her all night." Misty put her hand over her chest when she said this, like she was in disbelief.

"Okay, then tell us about your night."

Misty started right in. "When we got there, we all went down-stairs together. Cass and I went outside to listen to the band. We stood and talked to a couple of guys for a period of time."

Sam remembered looking down at the crowd and spotting Cassandra and Misty with two gentlemen fawning over Cass and making Misty look like some kind of subordinate.

Misty echoed her thoughts. "Those guys weren't interested in me. I stayed for a little while and listened to them ask all about Cassandra, and out of pity, I was brought into the conversation. I eventually got bored and decided to go get a drink. They probably didn't even notice I left. I wanted to find Paul and be entertained and maybe flirt a little." Her face flushed a crimson color when she said this. She knew Samantha was aware of her interest in Paul, so she wanted to be honest about her intentions.

"I saw Paul and Chris through the crowd and observed them talking to some girls. I watched for a while, hoping the girls would walk away because I didn't want to intrude on their conversation if they were trying to pick them up. I didn't want Paul to feel awkward with me there since we had been hanging out all week and he might feel obligated to talk to me. I stood listening to the band until I saw Paul walk away from those girls. I'm embarrassed to tell you what I did next, but I'm sure Cassandra may have mentioned it to you already." She paused, hoping Sam or Jake would bring up the fact she followed Paul back to the house.

Sam could hear the distress in her voice and helped her out. "She said you told her you went back to the house at one point."

"Yes. Like I said, I saw Paul walk away from the girls he was talking to and head for the beach. I wasn't sure where he was going, but I thought it was a brilliant idea, at the time, to follow him. I wanted to catch him alone, as not to have to interrupt him where I may not be wanted. It sounded logical at the time," she said and shrugged with disconcertion.

"I saw that he was heading toward the house at a sprint. I casu-ally walked that way too and came up on Scott and Kari on the beach sitting in the sand talking. I think I told them I left my cell phone or something back at the house and that's where I was heading. When

I got in the house, I basically stopped in the living room and wondered what the hell I was going to say when Paul came out and saw me standing there. I knew he was getting on his bathing suit because Scott told me that Paul had just ran passed them to change into his suit. I guess I could have acted like I was retrieving something, but I just wanted to get out before Paul saw me and suspected why I was really there. I kind of panicked once I realized that I could be rejected." Her eyes were staring at the floor, too embarrassed to look at the interviewees.

"Was there anyone else in the house, or did you hear anything going on?"

She looked back up at Jake and answered, "I didn't see anyone else in the house, and it sounded quiet. Strangely, I did think I saw somebody at the front door. I walked toward the door and peered out, but I didn't see anything. It must have been a shadow or my eyes playing tricks on me. When I realized no one was out there, I went out the front door and returned to the party. When I got back to the party, I was walking through the living room when Cass abruptly grabbed my arm and startled me. I told her why I was jumpy, and she said we both needed a shot. Megan then appeared and did a shot with us."

Jake interjected, "How was Megan acting? Did she say what she was doing before she saw you two?" Jake glanced at Sam to see if her expression changed when he asked about her friend. Sam didn't react in any way, not even a sideways glance, and Jake was relieved to see she could be impartial.

"She seemed a little put out and maybe said she was irritated, but don't quote me on that. Or maybe I just thought that since she exasperatedly agreed she needed a shot too. I don't think she said specifically why she was perturbed."

"Did you see the man Cassandra was talking to when she grabbed your arm? Did she point him out to you?"

"No. She took me by surprise. She did tell me he was a complete bore and not to look back to encourage him. I didn't. She led me to the nearest bar and was relieved to have lost him. After our drink, we headed downstairs where we saw Scott throwing darts. Megan said she was going to chill and watch him. Cass and I found Chris and Paul, and we all ended up leaving together. I guess it was Scott who found Jenni lying in their room, and Cass ran to get you guys. We were all in shock and frightened for her. No matter how cruel someone has treated you, you never want to see them hurt."

Misty said that last sentence very genuinely with sorrow in her eyes, yet she also had said she wanted to drown Jenni in the pool with a veritable assurance at one time, Sam thought to herself.

Samantha had told Jake all about Misty's inferiority complex, about Jenni conceding to Paul about Misty's average looks, which brought back a lot of anger and resentment from Misty's past.

Jake turned to Sam after Misty left the room. "You weren't kidding that everyone had some type of dissension toward Jenni, which could be a motive to want to knock her over the head with something heavy. Do you think that story about seeing someone at the door was anything with merit or a way to allege there could have been someone else at the house at that time?"

"Who knows? At this point, anything is possible."

"It doesn't look like anyone can be accounted for the whole time they were at that party. Anybody could have slipped away for fifteen minutes and have been the culprit. Hell, you even said that she pissed you off at one point. They could say you were so distraught about your break-up that you took revenge on the handsome married couple since she rebuffed your advances to talk about things." Jake got a kick out of saying this and poked Sam in the ribs to make her laugh.

"I'm too busy plotting my ex's death," she said impassively.

They both stared at each other with serious expressions then smiled knowingly to each other.

CHAPTER 33

PAUL WAS THE CONCLUDING member in the house left to talk to Samantha and Jake. They planned on going to the hospital after hearing his timeline to check on Jenni and speak with Scott privately. As it stood, Paul, Scott, and Misty were the three strongest suspects. Scott was a suspect because he was the husband, and you always have to look at the spouse, especially since they were having marital issues. The note left in his car to come back to the house definitely added wariness to his motive. Paul and Misty admitting they were at the scene of the incident around the time Jenni got hurt automatically placed them in dubiety.

There was no hiding the fact that Jenni and Paul had a patently venomous relationship. Their views were hardly ever analogous, and their exchanges usually weren't amicable. Paul was infamous for beleaguering most people, and Jenni always took it personally and would retort back and excoriate him. Her type of responses would inevitably egg him on to tease her exceedingly more than others. At first, Samantha thought he was just having a laugh and didn't really mean any harm, but a couple of times, they both used personal specifics that went below the belt that would be hard to forgive. She wasn't sure why or how their relationship turned out this way.

"Honestly, there's nothing I hate more than someone who constantly boasts about themselves." Paul acknowledged the animosity between Jenni and himself to Jake and Sam. "We didn't get along because I would call her out on her shit. Am I feeling bad about her being in critical condition? Of course I am. I never wished her dead. I just didn't enjoy talking to her because it was like swimming in the kiddie pool—too shallow to get anywhere interesting. She used her looks to manipulate men, and she treated others like they were beneath her."

Samantha interpreted his last comment as referring to Chris and Misty.

He continued, "I don't mean to sound cold about someone who needs help right now, but I'm being honest. You were staying in the house for the past week." He looked at Sam. "It's no secret that there wasn't any love lost between the two of us, and I'd be lying if I said otherwise."

Sam nodded. "Yes, you both seemed to know how to get under each other's skin."

Paul shrugged at this remark.

"Did you and Jenni get in a fight over paper and pen?"

"I guess Chris told you about that. It was strange, almost like she was lurking around while everyone was still sleeping. I was up having breakfast, and Chris came back to the house from being at Mia's, and we were talking. All of a sudden, Jenni sneaks up on us and asks where she can get pen and paper. I made a joke about her not knowing where the kitchen is because she can't cook, and she made a fat joke that I would obviously know where the kitchen is because of my big stomach, or something like that. Juvenile shit, really. One thing I've learned from being around Jenni is if you make a snide remark, it's guaranteed she'll come back swinging."

"Did you know what she needed the paper for?"

"Nope, I didn't ask, and she didn't say. Now that I think of it, that paper she retrieved from the kitchen was a blue tablet. I saw it in one of the drawers, so I told her where to find it. Scott had a blue note in his hand when I was getting a drink from the kitchen yesterday afternoon. It struck me weird because he came in and stood staring at all the clothes the girls had piled up in the living room. I joked to him about it, and he placed the note on top of one of the piles of clothes. I didn't think much about it at the time and still don't, but maybe the paper Jenni needed was for him."

"Whose pile of clothes did he put the note on?"

He looked at Samantha like that was a ludicrous question. "You're kidding, right? I have no idea whose clothes were whose. Do I look like Dolce or Gabbana?"

"Point taken."

"Tell us about going back to the house last night when you left the party."

"Sure, I jogged past Scott and Kari sitting on the beach."

"Did you find it odd that they were out there alone?"

"Not exceptionally. When I came back to the party, he was on the beach with Megan. I think the women feel comfortable talking to him and getting advice from him since he's married."

"What did you do when you got to the house?"

"If you must know, I went to my room and used the bathroom. Then I changed and did a couple of push-ups. You know, to make my muscles look more defined since I'd be seen in my bathing suit. I realized that was a lost cause and went to the kitchen and got a glass of water and some chips."

"Did you hear anyone else in the house during that time?"

"No, I had put on Pandora through my phone when I got back to the house. I was jamming to some AC/DC. At one point, I did think I heard someone, but I called out when I left my room and no one responded. I figured it was just typical noise from a house. I didn't see anyone and left. I probably was there a total of seven to ten minutes."

"You came back to the party from the beach access?"

"Yes, and that's when I saw Scott and Megan near the gulf. They looked like they were arguing. They didn't notice me, probably because I was covered by the shadows, but I could see it was them by the moon's reflection off the water."

"Why do you say they were arguing?"

"Well, I noticed them because I heard Megan scream, 'Really, really, Scott!' and she was flaying her arms, and Scott had his arms crossed looking down at the water. It was just my perception. I don't know what they were talking about, and it really wasn't my business. I had more pressing things going on, like seeing those women in their bathing suits, so I continued to the party."

"Did you ever think that Scott could be having an affair with one of these girls?" Jake asked pointedly.

"I never gave it much thought. Scott's never said anything inappropriate about any of them. All the girls have a penchant to flirt with him, but I think that goes back to what I said about him being safe since he's married and considered harmless. Plus, he's a good-looking dude. I can admit it."

"Did you see anyone else on the beach or when you came back to the party?"

"The reason I left the party was to get on my trunks to go in the hot tub with some—let's say—well-endowed girls. I really wasn't searching for anyone else or, for that matter, noticing other things going on at the party. My mission was accomplished when I saw the girls were still hanging out in the tub."

"Was Chris still there waiting on you?"

"No. I didn't see him there when I returned, but he wound up with us shortly after."

"How long after?"

"Let's see, I asked the girls if they wanted a drink, and I went to the bar and got us all some cocktails. I got in the tub, and Chris probably showed up ten minutes later."

"Do you think Chris has a weird obsession with Jenni?"

Paul looked a little disconcerted with this question. "Weird obsession? I think he liked her at one point in time and may still find her attractive, but he also thinks she has an arrogant quality that is not attractive. She has definitely taken advantage of his fondness, and it bugs the shit out of me, and I've told him she manipulates him, but he's a good guy."

Paul wanted to defend his best friend in case there was any notion that Chris could have possibly been stalking Jenni and then tried to harm her because he couldn't have her. Truthfully, he did think Chris's adoration was slightly misguided and peculiar, but he'd never let anyone know he thought that of him.

Once Paul left the room, Jake stood up and stretched. "I hope you were able to do your womanly thing and get other meanings from everything we heard." He teased her because she had referenced that comment as sexist earlier.

"After we talk to Scott, I will let my superpowers ignite and see what I can conjure up."

"That sounds sexy. Can I help ignite anything else inside of you?"

"Actually, you helped ignite my hunger. Do you want to stop and get some food before we head to the hospital?"

"Are you sure your hunger is just for food?"

"Jake, do you really get any action with these lines?"

"You'd be amazed."

"I already am."

CHAPTER 34

SAM WENT UPSTAIRS TO grab her purse. Megan was sitting on the bed staring at her phone. She looked startled when Sam came into the room.

"Didn't mean to scare you."

"You're fine. I just didn't hear you coming."

Sam stopped and looked at her earnestly. "Meg, what were you and Scott talking about on the beach last night?"

"I thought I already told you? We weren't talking about anything even worth remembering—how great the house is, how fun the fishing trip was for him. Why do I feel like I'm being questioned again?" Megan said defensively.

"I'm sorry. It's just that Paul mentioned he heard you yell at Scott and thought you might be arguing."

Megan looked uncomfortable. "What did he think he heard?"

"Something along the lines of 'Really, Scott, really.' He said he wasn't sure if it was an argument or not though."

Megan looked past Samantha toward the windows like she was trying to remember. She hesitated a minute and then replied, "That must have been when he was telling me about the fish he caught and some crazy story that was funny from their adventure. I think I was actually saying that in awe. It's funny how perception can get misconstrued."

Samantha nodded. She didn't entirely believe Megan's story, but she didn't know why she would lie about it either.

"We're heading to the hospital to talk to Scott and see how Jenni's doing. I'll be back later and let you know."

Sam grabbed her purse and phone. She decided to shoot Brad a pithy text of what was going on with the investigation. After she hit Send, she cursed herself. She was so used to telling Brad everything that she still always assumed he'd answer and be happy to hear from her. He had been ignoring any communication lately, and it was hard for her to conceive that this was the same man she had wanted to spend the rest of her life with. She never thought he'd ignore her. She always thought that if something happened between them, they'd still be friends and converse here and there. There was an inner voice reassuring her that he couldn't ignore this message. *Who could ignore this message? It's pretty intriguing stuff*, she thought as she made her way down the stairs. She put her phone in her purse when she saw Jake waiting for her at the door and realized she was being unprofessional by thinking of Brad at a time like this.

At the hospital, Jenni's parents and Scott were in the waiting room looking exhausted and distraught. Their faces were etched with lines of worry and concern. Jenni's parents had got in their car and sped to their daughter's side as soon as they got word of her condition. They resided in Tallahassee, which was only a two-hour drive to Destin. Jenni's mother told us Jenni was in surgery to have a decompressive craniectomy. A neurosurgeon had to remove part of her skull to relieve the intracranial pressure. She explained how worried they all were because this surgery was the last resort. It was a risky operation, but it was the only thing that would relieve the raised pressure to allow cerebral blood flow or else Jenni could die.

Samantha felt awful after hearing this news and hated to be the one to have to ask Scott if they could speak with him for a few minutes.

That was where Jake took control and stood up and very eloquently expressed his compassion and then asked Scott if he wanted to grab some coffee in the cafeteria.

Scott knew they were coming and actually felt relieved to get away for a bit to talk to anybody about anything instead of sitting there with his thoughts.

Jake went to get coffee for him and Scott and a Coke Zero for Samantha. Sam and Scott found a table in the cafeteria that was away from the other staff and visitors to get a little privacy. While they were sitting waiting on their drinks, she observed Scott as he raked his hands through his thick, dark, full head of hair. Even disheveled and exhausted, he looked handsome.

"How are you holding up?"

"You know what, I'm hopeful. If anything, Jenni's a stubborn woman who is a fighter." He gave her a little smile of reliance. "I'm extremely tired and fell asleep after Chris and Paul left. I had been drinking all night, and alcohol puts me to sleep. I can't wait to put this nightmare behind me."

Jake overheard the conversation and sat down and doled out the drinks. "Here's some caffeine to keep you awake."

"Thanks, man."

"Scott, what do you think happened last night?" Sam looked at him, intently searching for any abnormal body nuances. She was taught what to watch for when people lie or are hiding something.

"I wish I knew. I feel guilty as hell that I didn't know where my own wife was part of the night. When you've been with some-one for so long, you unknowingly take them for granted. Sometimes when you're socializing, you tend to have fun and not think of your significant other. I guess, since I'm always usually with her, that it's nice to have fun with the boys while she hangs with her girlfriends. I hate to think I could have helped her if I'd known she went back to the house." Tears started welling up in his eyes. "But then, I can't beat myself up over it because even if I did know she went back, I wouldn't have been there to help her, you know?" He looked at Samantha and Jake for reassurance.

"That's true. If she would have told you she was heading back and you wanted to stay, you still would have found her when you found her." Sam made logic out of his thoughts.

"Walk us through your night."

He took a drink from his Styrofoam coffee cup and put it down with a sigh. "My thoughts are a little scattered, but my recollection of the night started with the fellas and I putting our names down to play pool.

We were all getting drinks at the bar downstairs in the game room. Cass and Misty decided to check out the band. Jenni and Kari hung with us for a while, then I think they went to hear the band. Jenni kissed me and said she'd find me in a bit. She told me she wanted to go explore the place. I basically hung in the sports room. I'm a huge sports nut and love that type of thing. I wanted to play pool, throw darts, drink, and watch sports on TV, and it was all there at my disposal, plus the booze was free.

"Kari grabbed me at one point and asked me if I could talk to her in private because Justin was driving her nuts. She wanted to go somewhere where he couldn't walk up on us talking. I grabbed her hand and led her through the crowd to the beach. Kari is like a sister to me, and I'd do anything for her. During that time, Paul ran past us, saying he was getting his swim trunks on to get in the hot tub with some women. Kari and I were amused. Misty strolled past us a minute or two after Paul went by, and we assumed she was following Paul to the house. Then we walked back up to the party, and Kari was going to look for Justin. I had told her that Justin seemed like a good guy but maybe not her guy. I told her to have a good night and address the issue after the vacation. She agreed, and that was it with that. While we were walking up the boardwalk, Megan appeared out of nowhere and asked me to walk down to the water with her. Since we were right there at the access to the beach, I obliged. We chatted about our vacation thus far, and she went back to the party. I stayed out there five or so minutes more to just enjoy the sound of the waves crashing then headed back to the party. I went back inside and played darts, and at some point, Megan, Cass, and Misty came up to me, and Megan chose to sit and watch me throw, and Cass and Misty walked outside. Then we all left around one."

"Did you and Megan have any kind of heated debate where she might have yelled something at you on the beach?"

"No, no heated debate. Megan talks kind of loudly and she's easily excitable but no heated debate that I can recall."

"Did you see Megan walk back to the party or did she walk back to the house?"

Scott looked at both of them, silent in thought, and shook his head. "I honestly didn't watch her walk away. I presume she walked back to the party since I saw her later."

"How did you find your wife?"

"Well, Kari informed me when we were leaving that Jenni had left earlier not feeling well, so I expected her to be in bed. I don't think Kari or I thought it was strange that Jenni went back early since we've all been going hard for the past couple of days. You know, drinking and out in the sun all day can wear you down. I figured Jenni was just worn out. When we got back to the house, I went to our room to put on my swim trunks. I tried the lights, but they weren't working. I made my way to the bathroom and turned on the light there and changed into my suit. I then went to the bed to check on Jenni. I didn't see her and looked around the room and saw her lying on the floor. I felt so horrible I wasn't there to help her," he said plaintively.

Jake waited a moment before asking the next question, "Were you having problems in your marriage?"

Scott looked back and forth at Sam and Jake and was forthcoming. "It's hard to say yes when she's in critical condition, but yeah, we were fighting a lot and things weren't as good as they could have been. In any marriage, you're going to have ebbs and flows, but you still love that person."

"Paul mentioned, after the girls got back from shopping, he saw you put a note on one of the girl's pile of clothes when you came inside. What did the note say and who was it for?"

"Note?" he said, feeling his day-old growth of hair on his face. "Oh, that wasn't a note—it was a receipt. Jenni had accidentally picked up Cassandra's clothes receipt, and she asked me to lay it on her pile of clothes. I wasn't sure which one was Cassandra's pile, but I guess I put it on the right stack since she didn't ask about it."

"Are you sure it was just a receipt?"

"I didn't look at it, if that's what you're asking, but I didn't question it either."

"What did you think of the note that was left for you in your car to come back to the house last night around eleven-thirty?"

He shook his head looking confused. "I don't know what you're talking about. What note?"

Sam explained why she knew about the note. "Do you remember when Megan asked for your car keys to get her lip balm out of your car yesterday morning?"

"Ah, yeah," he said, slowly wondering where Sam was going with it.

"She found a note lying on your car seat asking you to meet back at the house at eleven-thirty."

"From whom?"

"We presumed your wife."

"Why would Jenni write me a note instead of just telling me to meet her back at the house? Are you sure she wrote it, and are you sure it was for me?"

"Can we go down to your car and see if the note is still in the middle console?"

"Of course." He reached into his pocket and retrieved his keys. He handed them to Jake.

Jake returned with the note in his hand and gave it to Scott. Scott read the note, and his face flushed slightly.

The note wasn't exactly as Megan recalled it to Sam and Jake. It did ask for a meet-up around eleven-thirty that night. The composer of the note reasoned that being on vacation made her want to touch Scott.

"I've never seen this. Are you sure it's for me?"

"Turn it over—it has your name on it. It was on your car seat with a pair of sunglasses. Is this not your wife's handwriting?"

"It doesn't look like hers, but I don't see my wife's handwriting a lot since everything is either through text or e-mail. She did tell me that Cassandra put my sunglasses back in my car but they weren't on the seat they were on the dash when I grabbed them that morning, and I didn't see this note."

Jake was quiet as they pulled away from the hospital. Then he said, "Megan put the sunglasses on the dash and the note in the console, right?"

"Yes."

"Do you think Cassandra wrote that note or Jenni?"

"I don't know. I guess we'll have to ask Cassandra."

CHAPTER 35

S AMANTHA STUDIED JAKE'S PROFILE before asking, "So what are you thinking?"

Jake's eyes were squinted either from the glare of the sun streaming through the windshield or from being deep in thought. "I'm not sure."

They were both momentarily silent, then Jake regurgitated what was on his mind. "Scott could have been lying about not getting the note in his car and not writing the note that he put on Cassandra's pile of clothes—if it was even a note. He could have just told us that Jenni gave him a receipt to put on Cassandra's pile since Paul saw him with it and Jenni can't tell us differently. Cassandra could have written the note found in the car and Scott could have replied to it.

"Or Megan, who we know saw the note, could have purposefully hid the note in the console where Scott wouldn't see it, since she isn't fond of Jenni and him together. She could have gone back to the house to confront Jenni later that night while she waited for her husband. Plus, she saw Jenni leave the party and knew where she was going."

He looked at her out of the corner of his eye to see if her face twitched while he was making her friend Megan the suspect. Sam just stared straight ahead with her eyes focused and her forehead furrowed. She was deep in thought, taking in what Jake was saying and reflecting on everything she heard today.

Jake continued, "Or Cassandra could have come back to the house and been confronted by Jenni and something could have pursued. You said Jenni was in her husband's car before you and Megan saw the note. She could have seen the note and knew Cassandra wrote it and left it there for her husband to see. This would be her way to confront both of them. There are a lot of possibilities concerning that note."

"Yes, this is true." Samantha nodded as if she were in a daze. "But what would be the reason Megan would want to confront Jenni? They didn't have any quarrels this past week, and although Megan didn't particularly like Jenni, she specifically told me she avoided any type of confrontation with her. She knew Jenni was spiteful and she was adamant about not wanting any conflict between the two of them. She even went out of her way to act like she left her lip balm in my car because she didn't want Jenni questioning her about what happened the night before."

"Why would she not want to talk about the night before unless she was guilty of something?" Jake looked at Sam with an inquiring eyebrow raised.

"Meg is very nonconfrontational. She'd rather elude an uncomfortable accusatory conversation than feel cornered by someone who is browbeating her. She knew Jenni was asking around about Cassandra's behavior, and Meg didn't want to get involved with the twisted commentary going through Jenni's mind about Cassandra's supposed attraction to her husband."

"Fair enough. Should we believe that Misty saw someone at the front door while lurking in the living room waiting for Paul? If we did believe that Misty really did see someone at the door, then there's the possibility they hid until she left and then they let themselves in the house. That person could have been any of the rest of them staying here."

"Except Scott and Megan, since Paul said he saw them on the beach talking when he left the house," Sam pointed out to Jake.

"Yes, true, if there was even anyone at the door."

Jake persisted with Megan being a plausible suspect. "Being the devil's advocate, Scott didn't see where Megan headed after their discussion. Megan had read the note and thought it was written by Jenni to her husband. She could have figured that Scott never saw the note since he was talking with her. Megan may have wanted to talk to Jenni about something and knew where she'd be. You say she doesn't like confrontation, but if she's the one broaching a discussion, maybe she had no qualms about talking to her in private. It gave her ample time to go back to the house and see Jenni and then return to the party.

"Scott's alibi isn't that great either since he claims he stayed out on the beach alone. It gave him a chance to head back to the house and meet whomever he thought left him that note, assuming he got it. Maybe the note was from Cassandra or someone else staying in the house. It's always a possibility that Scott is having an affair with someone and Jenni caught wind of it and confronted her husband. He got angry and hit her with something heavy."

Samantha nodded her head. "I guess anyone's a possible suspect when we don't know the time Jenni actually got hurt. We know she went back to the house around eleven last night. She wasn't found until around one. We presume she got hurt somewhere between eleven and twelve because those are the times when people can't be accounted for."

Jake pulled into the circular driveway of the house. He turned to Samantha and said, "I have some work to do back at the station. I'll follow up with you later." He grabbed her hand and squeezed it.

Samantha got out of the car, and while Jake drove away, she stood gazing up at the colossal beach house. She thought about the first time she saw the house and marveled at the exquisiteness and extravagant edifice, and now there seemed to be a clinging aura of ominous tones, causing the hairs on her arms to stand up.

She pulled her phone out of her purse to see if Brad had texted her back. There were no missed calls or texts. Her heart sank. Although ignoring all communication from Samantha had become Brad's practice, she still wanted to believe that he was that reliable guy that loved her and never wanted to hurt her. She was in denial that he could continue to be so callous, and she rebuffed the idea that he could keep on disregarding her when all she wanted was to maintain some sort of a friendship. She prayed he would eventually ruminate and realize being without her was worth working out the self-doubt that followed him throughout his life. She still held hope the perpetual wall of armor he relied on as an impediment for dealing with his insecurities, past heartaches, and disappointments would finally crumble.

She climbed the looming brick stairs to the front door. She put her hand on the knob of the door handle but paused before opening the door to survey the area. She peered in through the glass door and could clearly see all the way to the living room and the back windows. She glanced around the porch to see if there was a good spot to hide from someone coming out the door. There were places in the facade of the house that jutted out and could easily become a chasm to disguise oneself when the dark of the night shadowed the area. There was also a portico to the right connecting the house to the four car garage. The two columns on both sides of the walkway supporting the portico were bulbous enough to be able to miss someone standing behind it in the dark. The light wouldn't have been lit on this pathway since no one was using the garages.

Satisfied with her assessment of that facet of Misty's account of thinking she saw someone on the porch and knowing it was probable they could have hidden, Sam walked inside.

The house had a placidity that wasn't there that morning, and it made her a little uncomfortable. The feeling conveyed a portent, like the calm before the storm. She roamed to the back bay of windows and looked down to see Paul and Chris sitting by the pool. She wondered where the others were.

She and Jake never got a chance to stop and grab a bite to eat and she was famished. She went to the kitchen to see what she could scrounge together for a late lunch. Her head was in the fridge when Misty surprised her by saying hello.

Sam jumped a little. "Oh, shit. I didn't hear you come in."

Everyone was a bit on edge and easily spooked.

"Sorry, I was just upstairs resting. It was a long night. I think Justin and Kari are in their room. Cass and Meg went for a walk. How is Jenni?"

"She's in surgery, and this type of surgery can last several hours." Sam eyed Misty and thought she'd casually ask her about the note. "Did you see Cassandra with a blue tablet possibly writing a note?"

"I did see a blue notepad, and Cass put it away when we cleaned up the kitchen the other day. Look in the drawer next to the oven."

Sam pulled open the specified drawer, and on top of some miscellaneous pens and pencils was the blue tablet.

"Cass used it to write the grocery list the first day we were here, why do you ask?"

Sam didn't answer her question, "Oh, that's right. I knew I saw it but didn't know where it was put, thanks."

At that moment, Megan and Cassandra walked into the house and greeted Samantha and Misty.

"How was the walk?"

"It felt good to do something active and get out of the house. We've been texting with Scott and we're going to head to the hospital to be there for him at the end of Jenni's surgery. Chris and Paul are going to come, and I'm going to tell Kari and Justin. We're going to take a quick shower." Megan delivered this information to Sam and Misty.

"Sounds good to me. I'm ready whenever you guys are," Misty told the girls as she plopped down on the sofa.

"I've got some work to do here," Sam told Cass and Megan as she walked with them to their rooms.

"We figured, since you had just come from the hospital, that you wouldn't want to go back."

"Yes, I'm also so very tired. I'm going to lie down for a while."

Sam turned to Cassandra when they got to her bedroom door. "Can I talk to you for a second, Cass?" Megan figured Sam wanted privacy to discuss something with Cassandra, so she announced she was going to jump in the shower and continued to her room.

Cassandra looked at Samantha expectantly, waiting to hear what she wanted.

"I'm just curious, the night you stayed at AJ's and Jenni and I came home earlier, I saw Jenni come out of your room. She said that she had lent you a shirt and she was looking for it but couldn't find it. Did you borrow a shirt of hers?"

Cassandra looked at Sam quizzically. "She said *I* borrowed a shirt? That's weird. I don't think I've ever borrowed anything from Jenni."

Sam had a feeling this would be Cassandra's response. "Do you keep a journal or notes on events in your life?"

Cassandra walked into her room and welcomed Sam to come in. "I don't keep a journal, but I did bring my scheduler." She opened her suitcase and unzipped a side pocket. She held it up for Samantha to see. It was just an ordinary book-sized yearly scheduler of appointments.

"Would you mind if I look at it?"

"Sure, it's not private material. It's my meetings and work lunches that I have scheduled each month. No *Fifty Shades of Gray* here."

Samantha looked through the book and noticed that Cassandra's written *t*'s matched the note found in Scott's car. She hooked the bottom of the *t* where most people probably wrote their *t*'s like a cross. That didn't necessarily prove anything, she thought to herself.

"Did you write anybody a note asking to meet back at the house around eleven-thirty last night?"

Cassandra answered defensively, "Of course not. Did someone say I did?"

"No, no one said you did, but there was a note under Scott's sunglasses you put in his car."

"I put his sunglasses back in his car, but I didn't leave a note or see a note."

"Okay, I'll see you guys when you get back from the hospital." Samantha turned to head to her room and left Cassandra standing there looking confused. She didn't have an answer for Cassandra as to why Jenni had been in her and Misty's room, and she didn't know who wrote the note that was left in Scott's car. She walked quickly to her bedroom so Cassandra couldn't bombard her with questions she couldn't answer.

Samantha settled in her bed to get some much-needed sleep. She was glad the house was going to be empty for a couple hours. Megan came out of the bathroom to get dressed and Samantha asked her, with closed eyes, if everyone was planning on heading out tomorrow to go back to Atlanta.

Megan confirmed that since tomorrow was Sunday and technically the last day they were supposed to be there that yes, everyone was going to head back home.

Samantha figured they all would be leaving and she knew she'd have to head back too. She really hoped resting would rejuvenate her brain and something might come to her in her sleep.

CHAPTER 36

THE NEXT MORNING SAMANTHA got up early, poured a small glass of orange juice, and took it out to the porch to enjoy the peacefulness of the waking day. It was too early to have sunbathers lying on the beach, allowing the seagulls to take owner-ship of the pristine white coastline. She watched the lone morning walker following the outline of the tide's pattern left on the sand. Sam knew from growing up close to the beach that right where the tide reached the farthest to the sand was the most ideal spot to walk upon. The dampness of the current hardened the sand just enough to support your footing, whereas closer to the water the sand was too wet, producing your feet to sink with every step. Plus, the next wave would inevitably get your sneakers wet. She sighed deeply, knowing her call to Jake would vitiate the scene of this glorious paradise.

She reluctantly grabbed her cell phone and dialed Jake's num-ber. She told him her thoughts about the case and the conclusion she came up with last night. After they hung up, she waited patiently for the house to awake. She wanted to gather everyone together before they decided to take to the rode. She was apprehensive of what she had to reveal to the group since she was going off a capricious whim of what she believed happened to Jenni. Yet she was confident in her conjecture of what went down that night.

Scott was supposed to be heading back to the house early to gather and pack Jenni and his belongings. Jenni came through the surgery alive, but it remained an acutely sensitive time to make sure intracranial hematoma expansion didn't occur from the trauma of the surgery. They would not know the extent of damage that may ensue until she was out of the critical stage.

Out of the corner of her eye, Sam caught movement in the living room through the expanse of the windows and she glimpsed Scott walking swiftly to his room to gather his stuff. This was her cue to get prepared to congregate everyone before they leave the house to head back to Atlanta. She walked inside and glanced at the clock on the microwave. Jake was due to be there any minute.

Cassandra was the last to come downstairs tugging her suitcase behind her. She looked refreshed with her hair in a messy bun and was sporting a comfortable yellow sundress with matching wedge sandals. Looking at her, you'd never conceive that there was an attempted murder the night before and the suspect was in the room.

Most of the guests thought Jenni fell and hit her head, but Samantha was going to recite her theory on what actually happened the night Jenni got hurt by using the corroborated events that the others disclosed to Jake and herself in the library yesterday.

Samantha wanted her oration to the group to be conducted in a calm and casual manner instead of a salvo of accusations. What she was about to relay to the group would sound like denunciations, but she wanted it to be more of a barrage of possibilities that she used to deduce from to come to her conviction. Her plan was to address each member of the household in an insinuation of incrimination to carefully watch each person's nonverbal communication cues and mannerisms—a type of subterfuge. Her hypothesis of what went down that tragic night wasn't 100 percent fact, so Sam had to rely on her other abilities to assess how confident she felt her conclusion was of the calamity that took place.

Samantha stood in front of the group of people she had spent her vacation with and began her commentary. "I know we're all anxious to get home and get back to some kind of normalcy, but I wanted to discuss some things before everyone heads out. We are all aware that Jenni is still in critical condition, and we're all praying that the surgery brings a full recovery." She looked at Scott when she said this, and he nodded with appreciation for the sentiment.

"With that being said, Jenni did not accidentally fall. She was brutally hit over the head by some type of copious object." Sam looked around the room as she delivered this statement. Some of the faces looked back at her questioning while others stared at her with a look of shock and horror.

"I have gone over each person's account of their night, and I've come to some conclusions. As I go through the chronicle of events, please do not take offense when I point out motives each one of you could have had to do such a horrendous act—I'm just letting you know the process I went through to get to the final denouement." She paused to let her words sink in so they understood that they all would eventually be put on the hot seat.

"The first night at this beautiful beach house, Jenni accused Cassandra of essentially wanting her husband. I wasn't sure if this was just inebriated talk or if there was any substance behind her indictment. I found out that Cassandra and Jenni did have a convoluted past involving dating the same men, which still harbored resentment and dubious motives toward each other. Could Cassandra want to get the ultimate revenge on Jenni and go after her husband because Jenni took someone away from her in the past? I wasn't sure, but Jenni had spewed allegations about Cassandra and Scott the first night and this was obviously a concern of hers." Cassandra was sitting on one of the barstools, shaking her head.

Sam continued, "There were two notes written about meeting at the house around eleven thirty that fateful night. The first note was found lying on the driver seat of Scott's car. It basically suggested a rendezvous back at the house while everyone was still at the party. The note was originally thought to have been written by Jenni intended for her husband, but after the accident, I wasn't totally convinced of that scenario. I found the second note by happenstance, and it was signed with an *S*."

Scott interjected when he heard this information, "I didn't write any note. What note? What did it say?"

Samantha turned to Scott, "Like I said, it's going to sound like I'm accusing all of you at one point, so let me finish and it will all make sense."

"I'll get back to the notes and you, Cassandra." Sam looked at Cassandra to make sure she understood she would be brought up again.

"It took me a while to figure out who wrote the notes and who was originally supposed to receive them. My plan was to look at each person in the house individually to conceive if there was a motive to want to hurt Jenni. Let's face it, motives for killing someone can range from extremely vengeful to truly mundane circumstances."

She turned to look at Chris. "I'll start with Chris. I focused on your unique relationship with Jenni. It is obvious to most that Chris carries some inveterate feelings for Jenni, and he admitted to Jake and me, rightfully so, that he's still enchanted by her beauty. Adversely, Jenni took advantage of Chris's admiration at times and essentially used Chris's kindness to gratify her own egotism. I wondered if this display of selfishness was as apparent to Chris as it was to his best friend, Paul. Paul has admitted the main catalyst of his disdain for Jenni was how painfully obvious Jenni's control over Chris was due to his affection toward her. Could Chris have snapped? Did he finally have enough of Jenni's dominance over him without anything in return?"

Everybody turned slightly to look at Chris sitting on the sofa. His face showed a combination of fear from the accusation and from being mortified with the acknowledgement of his feelings toward Jenni.

"After Paul left to go back to the house to get on his swim trunks, Chris said he made his way upstairs and passed Megan on the way up the porch stairs. Megan verified this was true and told him Justin was on the porch. He said he didn't see Justin and just ate and watched the party from the porch alone. No one saw Chris for at least ten to fifteen minutes. Could he have changed his mind and went back to the house to change into his suit? Misty thought she saw someone on the front porch. Did he hide until Misty left then went inside and realized Jenni was in her room and they got in a heated fight that ended in him hitting her over the head?" Sam paused to ponder this plot.

"Highly unlikely. Chris didn't know Jenni went back to the house, and why would he have hidden from Misty if she saw him on the front porch? So I took Chris off the list of suspects."

Chris looked a little flushed by embarrassment from the admission of his doting behavior but also relieved that he wasn't going to be the topic for further discussion.

"That brings us to Paul's volatile relationship with Jenni. You've been very honest about your dislike of Jenni purely based on a disapproval of different life values and intentions." Sam remarked to Paul, as he nodded in agreement.

"Unfortunately, you were in the house during the same time Jenni was there, and earlier, you both had a verbal argument when walking to the party that we all witnessed. The argument went as far as you implying you would want her dead."

"Oh, please. I never said that," Paul countered.

"The conversation went something like she'd kill herself if locked in a room with you, and you asked for someone to lock you two up so she could go through with her threat."

"That was a joke."

"I'm just pointing out everything I had to take under consideration. Anyway, you said when you got back to the house, you went to your room to change and use the bathroom. This is why when Misty showed up, you didn't see each other and she decided to leave before you even knew she was there. Could you have found Jenni in her room and picked up where that argument was left off and this time it escalated to violence? This was a possibility. So I had to put you on the list of possible suspects, Paul."

Paul shrugged and said, "Okay. I've been on worse lists."

Sam turned to Misty. "You also went back to the house around the time when Jenni was there. You and Jenni had a somewhat cordial relationship, but this week, you had overheard some disparaging remarks that Jenni had said about you to Paul. Those words affected you deeply because they immersed with past insecurities that brought you pain and feelings of resentment.

"We know you followed Paul back to the house because you told us and Scott and Kari saw you also. The possibility"—Sam did air quotation marks when she said the word *possibility*—"that could have occurred is Paul went to change and use the restroom. He said he turned on his music so he couldn't really hear if Jenni came out of her room and if there was an exchange of words between the two of you. Jenni may have belittled you and made you feel inferior for following Paul back to the house for alone time. This may have triggered a belligerent reaction from you, propelling you to follow her to her room and hit her over the head. When you realized what you did, you placed her by the coffee table to make it look like she fell then raced out the front door to get away from the scene. You told Jake and me that the reason you left before Paul saw you was because you felt foolish and you felt vulnerable, when in reality, was it because you just hurt Jenni? You could have also made up the story that you thought you saw someone at the front door because you knew it would incriminate you and Paul unless there was someone else supposedly there too."

Misty's mouth was agape with a stunned expression on her face. Samantha knew Misty would be speechless and horrified with her account of the events that took place that night, so she continued, not to prolong her distress.

"Both these scenarios are credible, but it didn't explain that there were two notes written for some type of tryst to take place that night in this house, and I don't think the notes were meant for either Misty or Paul. I had a hunch that those notes had more to do with what happened to Jenni than just a confrontation of chance happening that night. Misty and Paul were mentally exed off my list."

"Oh my god, thank God," Misty blurted out. "I need to get a glass of water." She got up from the couch and staggered to the kitchen.

CHAPTER 37

Thave been in the car, so we assumed the note was written from her to her husband. There was a pair of sunglasses placed on top of the note. Cassandra admitted to putting the sunglasses back in Scott's car after having mistakenly grabbed them the night after coming home from the bar. Yet she denies writing or seeing a note addressed for Scott asking him to meet back at the house around eleven thirty that fateful night.

"Cassandra did write the grocery list on the same pad of paper the note was written, but Jenni also asked to borrow that pad to write something down. Like I said in the beginning of this discourse, Jenni had a preconceived conviction that Cassandra was after her husband. Although she would never admit her diffidence in her relationship with her husband, she did suspect Cassandra and Scott were having an affair. I asked Cassandra to see something that she had written to compare the handwriting of the note left in Scott's car to her penmanship, and they looked very similar. I'm not claiming to be a forensic document examiner, but a lot of the letters were crafted the same way."

Sam looked at Cassandra. "Judging the handwriting, I would have assumed you wrote the note left in Scott's car. I also noticed that a page of your planner was ripped out. I wasn't sure if you were

180

trying to hide something. I knew if I asked about it, you probably wouldn't confide in me about an illicit meeting you didn't want anyone to know about so I stored that information away." Cassandra's eyes enlarged when Sam said this.

"Cassandra told Jake and me that she was in an in-depth conversation with a man for a length of time during the critical hours we are investigating, yet she couldn't remember his name. When Misty got back to the party, she was confronted by Cassandra about a boorish man she got stuck talking to, and she ordered Misty not to turn around to look at him because it might encourage him to approach her again. Did this man really exist? Or did Cassandra really slip away from the party on account of meeting Scott at the house around eleven-thirty? Since Jenni saw the love note, did she plan on meeting Cassandra back at the house to confront her? Cassandra could have walked into Scott's room and been so overwhelmed by finding Jenni in the bed instead of Scott that out of desperation, she hit Jenni over the head. She could have been slinking out the front entrance when Misty caught a glimpse of someone on the porch. Back at the party, she immediately grabbed Misty and told her about some faux verbose man she'd been trapped listening to, which built an alibi for herself. She stated she needed a shot after dealing with this man, or was the truth really, she needed a drink to calm her nerves after maliciously hitting Jenni over the head and leaving her lying on the floor to die?

"I estimated that this scenario is plausible while trying to assess what happened that night but then wondered what role Scott played, and was he present with Cassandra in the bedroom? Maybe Cassandra went to meet Scott and they were both present with Jenni, but could it have been Scott that got inflamed and hurt his wife?

"Jenni was feeling insecure with Cassandra's relationship with her husband, as we all heard her accuse Cassandra of yearning for Scott. I did witness Cass and Scott out in the ocean, frolicking on boogie boards catching waves and having a good time together. It could have been innocent enough, but there could also have been more to it. I don't know. I wasn't down there with them, and I just spotted them from my bedroom balcony.

"Also, Paul saw Scott put a note on one of the piles of clothing while he was in the kitchen getting a drink. I asked Scott about what Paul had seen, and he claimed that Jenni had accidentally picked up Cass's clothing receipt and she asked him to lay it on Cassandra's clothes pile. Except it was more than a receipt. I found the note, and it asked the recipient to leave the party and meet back in *my* bedroom around eleven-thirty. This note was signed with the letter *S*. There was no other name on this note unlike the note in Scott's car that was addressed with his name. I obviously couldn't verify with Jenni if, in fact, she handed her husband a receipt of Cassandra's to be delivered. Scott could have made that up since Paul saw him put something on one of the piles of clothes. That made me make the conjecture that possibly Scott went back to this house after talking to Megan on the beach. Cassandra was already gone because she was accosted by Jenni and she fled back to the party. Scott showed up to find his wife waiting for him, and they got in an altercation about his fidelity and Scott hit her with something heavy out of frustration or guilt.

"Now I have a dilemma about who could have done this, Scott or Cassandra. I searched the house looking for clues last night while everyone was at the hospital. That's when I found the second note. It was in the trashcan of the guest bathroom in the hall off the living room. The note was crumpled up inside a Gap shopping bag, and there were two clothing receipts also in the bag. I presumed both receipts belonged to Cassandra because of all I had postulated about the note left for Scott. Still, I asked Megan about the receipt to be fair and to see if it could be her bag, but she said it wasn't hers. Next, I asked Kari if the receipt was hers, since I had seen her before the other two girls. She identified one of the receipts and bag as hers. I explained I was dumping the trash and it fell out and I wanted to make sure she didn't need it, which isn't entirely untrue." Sam looked over at Kari and shrugged. Kari furrowed her brows and frowned, contemplating where this narrative was heading.

"That put a new equation to the story. Maybe I had it wrong with Cassandra. Why would the second note be in a bag that belonged to Kari? I thought back to Cassandra's interview, and she told us that she had overheard Scott and Jenni arguing over Scott coming home from work late. Cassandra heard Jenni ask her husband if he was having an affair. Last night, I was thinking about this admission, and it struck me as odd to disclose this conversation if Cassandra was, in reality, having an affair with Scott. If Cassandra was truly having an affair with Scott, would she tell us she overheard his wife accusing him of it? I didn't think so."

Sam turned to address Cassandra. "Plus, you said you teased Jenni about Scott's sexy moves on the dance floor to get under her skin. I don't think you would bait her like that if behind the scenes, you're actually having an affair with her husband. Cassandra, I ruled you out of being a suspect."

Jake stepped forward. "Plus, Sam, I know you don't know this yet, but we narrowed it down and found the guy Cassandra spoke with around eleven-thirty. He confirmed her alibi this morning."

Samantha let out an internal *Thank God*. She wasn't a hundred percent certain in any of her conclusions, but she only hoped her final psychoanalysis proved true.

CHAPTER 38

J AKE NODDED HIS APPROVAL to Samantha and gestured for her to continue. Samantha was ready to conclude her thesis of what she really thought happened to Jenni that night. So far, all the reactions from the alleged suspects were what she predicted and anticipated, and it made her feel more confident about her final hypothesis.

"What did finding this note in Kari's bag imply? Was it really Kari and Scott who were having an affair? Kari was the closest to Jenni, which meant she spent a lot of time around Scott. Many love affairs occur because of the comfort and time shared with someone. Jenni trusted Kari with Scott, and she would often use Kari's familiarity with Scott to bid him away from Cassandra. It was Jenni who encouraged Kari to jump on Scott in the pool while he was talking to Cassandra and to dance with him at the bar when she went home. Did Jenni unknowingly push her husband and friend together while trying to discourage his involvement with Cassandra?

"I noticed that Justin was aware of Kari's interactions with Scott, and he wasn't too appreciative of it. He's a quiet guy and probably never mentioned to Kari that he wasn't too keen with some of her behavior toward Scott, but it was obvious and written all over his face—at least to me.

"Kari was with Jenni last at the party before Jenni headed home. If that note was meant for Kari, she could have freaked out that Jenni was going back to the house when she was supposed to meet Scott there. Did she follow Jenni home and things ensued? Or is that why

Kari found Scott and they went out to the beach to privately discuss that Jenni was back at the house? Scott and Kari both said they were out on the beach talking about Kari's troublesome relationship with Justin. Only they know what was really being discussed, so who knows if Justin was the actual topic of conversation? I wasn't quite sure of anything yet.

"I needed to focus on the two notes. If Kari was involved, why would she blatantly put the note on the seat of Scott's car where others may see it? Everyone knew the men were going fishing early that day, so whoever put it on Scott's car seat did it that morning, hoping only Scott would see it. When would Kari get the chance to put it out there if Cassandra didn't see it there when she put back the sunglasses?

"Meg and I saw the note shortly after Cassandra put the glasses in the car, and the only other person that could have written the note and put it on the seat was Jenni. Jenni was so consumed by the possibility that Scott was having an affair that she staged a meetup for her husband so she could see if he'd show up. She must have concocted this plan the night we came home from AJ's. I found her coming out of Cassandra's room, and she told me she was looking for a shirt she had let Cassandra borrow. I asked Cassandra yesterday if she ever borrowed a shirt from Jenni, and she denied ever doing so. I also asked Cassandra if she had anything personal in her room like a journal or diary. She handed me her day planner and said it was just business appointments that were recorded in the book. I glanced through her planner and noticed a page missing. At the time, I wasn't sure why Cassandra would have ripped out a page in her planner, and thought it possibly had something incriminating on it. Then I remembered Jenni had been in Cassandra's room probably looking for something to link Cassandra to her husband. When she couldn't find anything of importance to connect Scott with Cass, she decided to construct a note to her husband, presumably by Cassandra. She used the page she ripped out of Cassandra's planner to mimic her handwriting in case her husband could recognize Cassandra's penmanship or her own. Hence why I thought Cassandra wrote the note addressed to Scott—because the letters were composed in the same fashion. To verify my assumptions, I searched Jenni's room. As I suspected, I found Cassandra's ripped-out calendar page in Jenni's book on her nightstand.

"Early in the morning, Jenni woke up, ready to create the plan that materialized in her mind the night before. She probably didn't expect Paul and Chris to be up so early. Instead of rummaging through things, she asked them where she could find a notepad and pen to compose the now-infamous note to look like Cassandra's handwriting. Jenni had just put the note in her husband's car when Megan and I walked outside to retrieve Meg's Chapstick. Jenni seemed startled to see us, but when she saw we were getting something out of my car, she retreated inside to shower for their shopping trip. Megan found the note on Scott's seat and read it. She and I discussed that it must be a love note from Jenni setting up a rendezvous with her husband to try to spice up her marriage. Meanwhile, Meg distractedly put the note inside the middle console when she retrieved her Chapstick.

"Scott did get his sunglasses out of his car that morning before they left to go fishing, just like Jenni knew he would, but the note was now in the center console and not in plain sight, where Jenni had left it.

"It was a shrewd plan of events since Cassandra did put Scott's sunglasses back in his car so one would assume she also wrote the note. Unfortunately for Jenni's plan, her husband never saw this note, and it remained in the console of his car unread.

"Jenni was also the author of the second note. This plan, too, didn't go the way Jenni intended. She must have thought long and hard how she wanted this note delivered. It would have been brilliant if Scott was actually paying attention when Jenni was giving him a fashion show." Sam saw the confusion on everyone's faces.

"Let me explain. Jenni could have left that note in Cassandra's room or in her purse, but she wanted to make sure Cassandra actually saw the note and it was delivered by the supposed composer. I believe Scott when he told us Jenni explained to him she had accidentally picked up Cassandra's receipt and asked him to put it on top of her clothes. She most likely believed that Scott was attentive while she showed him each item she purchased."

Samantha stopped and turned to Cassandra. "Do you remember whose clothes pile was next to yours?"

Cassandra thought back about it and answered, "Jenni's."

"That's what I thought," Samantha said.

Sam continued with the dissection of her theory. "Jenni would have told Scott to put the note on top of Cassandra's pile, which was right next to her clothes, yet she didn't take into account that Scott couldn't identify which pile was hers so it was impossible for him to know which pile was Cassandra's. Instead, he guessed and put the note on top of Kari's clothes." Sam stopped to let it all sink in.

"Paul witnessed Scott putting some paper on someone's clothes yet neither knew whose clothes were whose. Scott didn't bother to ask Paul which pile was Cassandra's because he knew he wouldn't know either. It would have been like the blind leading the blind. Scott just picked a clothes pile and disposed of the receipt, like he was told to do.

"That momentous night, Jenni feigned that she wasn't feeling well so she could get back to the house before her plan unfolded. I noticed when Jake and I entered her room and tried to switch on a light, no light came on. I found the bulb in the drawer under the light that the wall switch was connected to. Curious, I went over to the closest nightstand and tried to turn on the lamp sitting upon it and once again this lamp did not work either. Again, I found the bulb in the nightstand drawer. However, the lamp on the other side of the bed did work, and this is where Jenni was positioned under the covers waiting. I believe Jenni disabled the other lights in order to control the situation. She expected either Scott or Cassandra to show up, and she wanted them to have to walk in the room and call out each other's name, and this would validate to Jenni why they were there. Then she could turn on her light and confront whoever showed up first."

Samantha paused and looked around the room. All eyes were on her except the person she was about to accuse of attempted murder. This solidified what she knew happened, so she forged ahead with her account.

"Did Kari show up? No. Kari never saw the note because it was Justin who took her clothes back to her room for her. I remember specifically because I complimented him for being so thoughtful to clean up Kari's belongings. I guess it's true that no good deed goes unpunished.

"Justin was feeling insecure about Kari and Scott's relationship. He didn't approve of the way she laughed and palled around with him, and finding this note justified his suspicions. I'm presuming after he read the note, he joined us on the porch when Kari was playing tune in Tokyo with Scott and then hugged him. I saw a flash of a menacing look glimmer in Justin's eyes when he saw this interaction, almost the same look I noticed he gave them at the pool. He recovered quickly when Kari drew attention to greet him.

"Before the party, Kari told us Justin was insecure and enraged about what she was wearing and asked if they could stay home. She was beginning to get frustrated at Justin's lack of amity with the other guests and his constant detest of sociable gatherings. She refused to succumb to his antagonistic attitude and disregarded his argument. This probably added fuel to his already preconceived idea that Kari was messing around with Scott. At the party, Kari admitted to us she was avoiding Justin and basically hiding from him.

"Justin, you said you were on the upstairs porch looking over the crowd to find Kari and you saw her walking toward the beach with Scott. In Scott's interview, he told us the same account, but he mentioned he grabbed Kari's hand to help her through the crowd. Now, after you read that note and then seeing Kari leaving the party with Scott *and* holding his hand, you had no doubt that they were going back to the house to have an affair. Your temper got the best of you, and you flew out the front door and headed back to the house to confront them. I know this because Megan saw you on the porch overlooking the party when she was heading for the steps. She passed Chris on the stairs and mentioned you were by yourself on the porch and she told him to go join you. Chris said he immediately went to look for you, but he never saw you up there. The reason he never saw you up there is because you left the party, isn't it? Chris was up there for a while eating and drinking and would have seen you if you were there."

188

Samantha noticed Justin's cold stare penetrating her as she glanced at him. She didn't care that he was trying to intimidate her. She knew what he was capable of, and she was going to expose him. She locked eyes with him and continued with her monologue.

"When you got to the house, you could see Misty standing in the living room through the glassed doors. You swiftly moved to the shadows and hid when she came out the entrance. You watched her return to the party and waited to go back in the house. The note you found said to meet in Scott's room, so that's where you headed. You surreptitiously entered the bedroom. You tried the switch by the door, but no light came on. You continued to penetrate farther into the dark room, and Jenni called out Scott's name because she could hear a presence in the room. You were filled with rage at this point and concluded that it was Kari asking for Scott. You picked up the coral centerpiece off the coffee table when you passed the sitting area and moved toward the bed. Your anger got the best of you, and while Jenni turned to switch on her bedside lamp, you lifted the coral design piece and maliciously came down with brute force to hit her on the side of her skull with the heavy block of wood the coral was mounted to. The light illuminated the room, and you discovered it was Jenni slumped over in the bed from your malign impact."

There were some gasps that permeated the room. Kari couldn't even bring herself to look at Justin. She continued her shocked, wide-eyed stare at Samantha, waiting to hear what she would say next. Samantha figured she was probably in a stupor and was trying to process what was being said. Sam had speculated and was right that Scott wouldn't attack Justin. She knew there was a part of him that felt guilty about some of the circumstances that led up to this incident, and he was trying to digest the occurrences. Sam wasn't going to reveal that guilt to the group.

Samantha continued, "Justin knew he had to do something to make it look like Jenni wasn't attacked. He picked her up out of the bed and staged her by the coffee table to make it look like she fell. He retrieved a towel and proceeded to wipe the base of the coral he used to hit her with and then placed the towel by Jenni's feet to pose as the catalyst to the fall. He ran back to the party to find Kari.

"After Chris was done eating and was in line to use the bathroom, he finally spied Justin in the upstairs living area in what he described as a frantic state. Justin was fraught because of what he had just done to Jenni, and he desperately needed to find Kari to establish an alibi.

"Kari also told us Justin seemed upset and frantic when she saw him, but she attributed his behavior from being left alone in a social environment. When in truth, he was distraught about the potential fatal blow he had just administered to Jenni."

Justin's face turned ashen with fear. His stance was still rigid as if he were listening to his commander barking orders for a military training exercise, except his eyes darted around the room at everyone ogling him.

"You made one big mistake. You forgot to pull down Jenni's pajama pants after taking her out of bed. I knew when I looked at her lying there that she couldn't have walked across the room and fell when the legs on her pajamas were raised up from being under the covers in the bed."

"I would never hurt anybody," he said in a wavering voice. "I'm the harmless, shy guy. I'm not capable of such actions."

Samantha dismissed Justin's declaration about himself. "Justin, I spoke to your ex-wife Heather, and she conceded that there was physical abuse in your marriage. Although she never officially filed against you; the police were called on occasion. When the Navy Seals brought up your ex-wife in your interview, it made you anxious and agitated because you weren't sure what they knew about that relationship. It cost you entry into that program because you showed too much emotional affliction. You do come across very mild-mannered, but there's a fierce temper inside you with a jealous rage. At least that's how Heather described you. You're a lot different than what you normally betray and how most of us saw you."

Kari finally had the nerve to turn to Justin and confront him on what she just absorbed about him. "Why, Justin, why would you do that? You thought that was me in the room." She had a fearful look on her face.

"I thought you were cheating on me. I didn't want you to leave me."

"Instead you were going to kill me?" Kari looked at Justin horrified.

"Oh my, God, no. I wouldn't do that. I was just upset and—" Justin never finished his sentence because Jake came up and grabbed his arms around his back to cuff him and started reading him his Miranda rights as he led him out the door to his patrol car.

Justin looked desperately over his shoulder while Jake forcefully led him outside. He hollered, "Kari, you know I would never really hurt you or anyone. It was an accident. It was because I love you. You made me do this."

Samantha walked outside to say goodbye to Jake while the rest of the group stayed stunned and silent in the living room. Jake was putting Justin in the back of his cruiser when Sam came out the front door.

"You brought the patrol car. I guess you had faith in my assessment."

"I didn't doubt you for a second. When you called this morning with your version of what happened, I was totally on board. I wasn't too sure about a confession, but you nailed it when you predicted how he would react. You must charge a lot for therapy." He gave her that cocky grin she loved.

"Ha! I've studied enough personality characteristics to make estimable assumptions of behavioral norms, but I'll tell you, after every criminal case I've helped with, it still shocks me how human behavior is very unpredictable. I guess it's good that I still can't fathom how people are responsible for such hideous acts. When I'm not fazed by depravity and evil is when I'm going to worry."

"Yep. Life is very unpredictable." He grabbed her hand. "I wish we could have hung out under different circumstances." There was an awkwardness that they both could feel. He was on duty, and Justin was in the backseat of the car. Sam quickly gave him a hug and a kiss on the cheek.

"Call me later about the case."

"Will do."

Samantha turned to walk away and Jake called out to her. "Sam,"—she turned toward him—"thank you."

Samantha smiled and waved goodbye.

CHAPTER 39

ON THE WAY BACK to Atlanta, Samantha was settled in the passenger side of her car with the seat reclined so she could relax and stretch out. Megan was driving her vehicle, and Sam was enjoying the lull of the quietness and gentle motion from the velocity of the car. It had been a whirlwind the last couple of days, and Samantha was mentally exhausted from the energy she put into establishing what really happened the night Jenni was hurt.

They had just passed through Niceville and continued traveling on obscure rural backways. Samantha wasn't even sure of the town they were cruising through, but she trusted that Megan would not get lost as she shut her eyes.

Megan had something on her mind, and she finally blurted out, "You know, don't you?"

Samantha slowly opened her eyes, glanced over at her friend, and saw the torment in her expression. *I guess I'm not going to get a nap,* she thought to herself. She pushed the button on the side of her seat to an upright position. "Yes, I know."

"How did you figure it out and why didn't you expose us?"

"I'll tell ya, Meg, you didn't make it easy on me with this investigation. After I figured out Scott was having an affair with you, I had to really concentrate on the two of you as the main suspects. Maybe it helped me work harder to prove you didn't do it. I searched the house up and down while y'all were at the hospital to find some kind of evidence to prove your innocence. Jake wanted me to focus solely on you and Scott, and he was worried I wouldn't be objective enough to pursue an unbiased investigation. You were the only one who had slight inconsistencies with some of the things you told us."

"I did? What did I say that was inconsistent?"

"The first discrepancy was when you passed Chris on the porch stairs at the party. You told us you asked Chris if he had seen me. You said Chris told you no, yet Chris told us he specifically pointed where Jake and I were standing. Chris also mentioned that you asked where Scott was first. After he told you he didn't know the where-abouts of Scott, I'm assuming you asked where I was as to not create any suspicion about you and Scott. You were indifferent about his response where I was hence not remembering he pointed out where I was standing. Right?"

Samantha looked at her friend for validation. Megan remained silent and kept her eyes on the road but nodded in agreement.

"Then Paul said he heard you yelling at Scott on the beach although he wasn't sure why, and when you headed back to the party, Cassandra said you were irritated. You denied both of these allegations as misperceptions. I believed that could possibly be what they were—misperceptions. Cassandra also said that the night you came home from AJ's, you told her you went to bed shortly after she went up to bed. In reality, you didn't make it up to our room until I was already up and heading out to go on a morning walk. You told me you fell asleep on the couch. Cass also heard Jenni reprimanding Scott for spending the night on the couch that same night. But I had to look at more than what we were told by the others. You were very complimentary toward Scott when talking about him. The first night, you went downstairs to console him after his wife accused him of cheating. Plus, I thought it was strange how concerned you seemed when Scott and Cassandra were boogie boarding together. These instances are all circumstantial, but what really made me think twice was when I saw you returning to the house with Scott when you were supposed to be at the beach. I know how Type A you are about things, and when you said you left for the beach without your phone and that's why I saw you and Scott coming back to the house, I knew something was dubious. I saw you pack your beach bag that day and you had put your phone in the inside pocket. You expected me to be long gone with Mia to the outlets, but Mia was late showing up. I probably wouldn't have noticed Scott's vehicle passing me, but he turned without using his blinker, causing the car in front of me to slam on his brakes. You know how I hate when people don't use their indicators when turning, and that's why I noticed Scott's car and you were the passenger."

"I'm so embarrassed, and I feel horrible. If it was that obvious to you, do you think others suspect the same?"

"Meg, it wasn't that obvious. Jenni was positive that her husband was having an affair with Cassandra, not you. That's why she planned the secretive meetup." She paused and hesitated to ask Megan something instead of accusing her, but she was pretty certain of the answer. "You purposefully put that note in Scott's console, hoping he wouldn't see it, didn't you?"

Megan sighed. "Yes. I thought Jenni was trying to be romantic with Scott, and I didn't want him to be with her. I'm so stupid. After seeing how insecure she was acting and clinging on to him, I was afraid he'd fall back in love with her."

"And the reason you acted like you left your Chapstick in my car was because you were afraid that any suspicion Jenni had and aimed it at you would make you so uncomfortable that you might have given it away just by the expression on your face."

"Exactly. How did you know? I was terrified that she might accuse me of being with Scott and I would break down."

"I know you, Meg. That's precisely what would have happened, so you avoided any confrontation you could with Jenni."

Megan had tears rolling down her cheeks. Sam knew she felt responsible for Jenni's condition and felt guilty about her actions of betrayal.

"Sam, you could have exposed Scott and me. What made you not tell this part of your investigation?"

"The number one reason is because you are my friend. I was trying hard to clear your name off the suspect list. Do you really think I wanted to disclose your and Scott's indiscretions? Secondly, there's a woman who is in critical care and may not fully recover. I don't think it will do her any good to learn of Scott's infidelity. There was no purpose in the others knowing about the affair and chastise you and Scott for contributing to Jenni's accident. I don't condone what you did, but you had no way of knowing there was a sociopath in the house who has a low threshold for a discharge of violence."

Megan was visually upset about her selfish actions that had caused someone to be recklessly hurt. She tried to explain her conduct to Samantha. "I've always been attracted to and fond of Scott. When he started showing me attention and flirting back, I almost went delirious with elation. I didn't think any further than the pleasure he brought me. I was truly being self-indulgent, and I never took Jenni's feelings into consideration. Every chance I had, I insulted Jenni's ungracious behavior to justify my immorality. I wasn't thinking correctly, and now she's hurt and it's my fault."

"Why were you and Scott arguing at the beach that night?"

"That's the kicker to this madness. He said we shouldn't see each other anymore. He was feeling bad that Jenni suspected something, and he didn't want to continue to hurt her like this. He wanted to try to make his marriage work, and he said he was going to suggest counseling to her. Of course, this made me upset and incredulous about what he was telling me. I felt betrayed, yet I was the other woman. I was mostly mad at myself for getting involved with a married man." Megan was choking back sobs.

"Meg, I'm sorry all of this happened. I'm your friend and I'm going to be here for you. We all make stupid mistakes in the game of love. Look at me, I can't seem to shake a man who obviously doesn't love me enough to want to marry me, yet my heart doesn't give up the love for him. He's probably sleeping with another woman, but the thought of me with another man makes my skin crawl. That thought alone should make me move on, but it doesn't. Love is tough and hard and makes us shortsighted."

"I know you've been sad a lot and my heart aches for you, but I caused innocent people to get hurt."

"Meg, Kari was about to end things with Justin after this trip. He was a ticking time bomb and probably would have hurt Kari after she delivered the news. It's unfortunate that Jenni was the victim of his rage, but it's just like anything else tragic that happens in life."

"Thanks for protecting me."

They rode in silence most of the way back to Atlanta, both caught up in thoughts of heartbreak and sorrow. Samantha never heard back from Brad, and it confused her how someone that was her whole world could be gone in a way that felt like she was never significant to him and now was a total stranger.

CHAPTER 40

LIFE, AS NORMAL, CARRIED on for Samantha back in Atlanta. She spoke to Jake a couple times on the phone, but mainly it was about the case against Justin. They both were not looking for a long-distance romance yet knew what they had recently experienced in Destin would bond them in a different way than before. There was a mutual respect and trust with an undercurrent of flirtatiousness, but above all, a friendship.

At work, Bridget teased her about Detective Jake Johnson and her missed opportunity to take a ride on the cowboy.

"I just love that story that you used to call him Jake 'the Cowboy' Johnson. You were so close to finding out if your high school crush was what you always thought he would be."

"You know, they always say it's never as good as you think, so it's probably better to stay a mystery. Now I'll still have the memories of the schoolgirl crush intact."

"Yeah, you're right. I just wanted to live vicariously through you instead of the world where my husband and I are too exhausted to do anything after feeding the kids, giving them baths, and reading them bedtime stories. I sometimes wake up in the middle of the night in my child's bed and don't remember drifting off to sleep. I can't remember the last time my husband and I had wild, passionate sex. Hell, I can't remember the last time we kissed," she said with a laugh.

"I'd trade my love life with yours in a second. I'm at the age where wild, passionate sex isn't the top priority on my list for potential husbands. Yes, it would be nice, but if I'm in love, the sex never has been an issue. I miss having a companion and my best friend."

"I know you do. You're right, I shouldn't complain. I'd rather you find a nice guy that wants to give you everything than a hot fling. If I want to live vicariously through someone, I'll just watch porn."

"There you go!"

"Are you doing anything fun this weekend? Maybe I shouldn't ask—the last time I asked you were heading on vacation and someone almost died."

"I guess we can jest about it now since Jenni is doing well. They should be coming back to Atlanta this week, and Jenni will be monitored by doctors and therapists here. She is slowly regaining her memory but doesn't recall what happened that fateful night. This weekend, I'm sticking to what's safe and going to see my parents. I haven't been able to see them since I've been home because they went on vacation the week after I got back. I'm heading their way to fill them in on my vacase."

"Vacase?"

"Vacation and attempted murder case."

"Cute. Well, I'm not going to chastise you for hanging with Dan and Brenda any more. It's probably best you don't branch out and put any other potential friends in jail."

"Cute," She taunted her colleague back.

Bridget smiled. "I kid only because we have to in this profession. If we couldn't tease each other, we'd become as neurotic as our patients."

"I totally agree. I use you as folly as much as possible," Samantha told her friend as a joke but also meant it.

"You're welcome. Oh, speaking of patients, I had a really handsome man come in for a session while you were gone. I could set you two up?"

"He's a patient!"

"He's *my* patient, not yours. There's nothing wrong with that."

"Why is he coming to see you?"

"I can't tell you that. That's client confidentiality," she said with a laugh.

"Funny. I'm a psychologist who is your partner—you can tell me."

"Fine, but you can't judge him. I won't say his name. He's suffering from self-esteem issues."

"Beeecaauuse…" Sam tried to pry more information.

"Because he's experiencing erectile dysfunction," Megan responded nonchalantly.

Sam rolled her eyes. "Oh, yes, Bridget, sign me up," she said sarcastically. "No, forget it. I have enough to worry about then to cater to a guy whose ego is stuck in his pants."

"You said you didn't care about sex at this stage of your life. You've been celibate since Brad and it's been almost a year. This shouldn't even faze you."

Samantha laughed and grabbed her purse to head out the door.

"Thanks, B, but if I'm going to be celibate, it's going to be because I'm alone. You and I both know how much a man equates everything in their lives to how their penis functions."

"Just trying to help. Think about it. Tell Dan, the man, and Brenda I said hello."

Sam called out, "No and will do," as she headed out the door.

CHAPTER 41

As Samantha pulled up to her parents' house, she immediately felt a sense of security and peace. Even though this was not the home she had grown up in, there was a comforting feeling when you knew the two people living in that house supported and loved you more than anyone else in your life. After her upheaval of a vacation, it felt good to be around people you could always trust and who had your back.

Samantha walked right in the front door without knocking. She knew her parents would be out back on their porch enjoying the nice weather. They practically lived out there and even bought a standing propane outdoor heater for when it gets chilly.

There's almost a cheer of hellos when Samantha opened the backdoor and stepped onto the porch. She instantly saw there was a martini with three olives waiting for her.

"I see you remembered the deal," she said as she pointed to the drink.

"Of course I did. Did you expect anything less?"

Sam knew her father would remember. He was the only man she's ever met that was as good as a host as her mom. He actually noticed when people needed refills and would jump up to refresh drinks and liked to put snacks out too.

"Now sit down and tell us what happened."

"Your father has been dying to hear this story and talked about it incessantly during our vacation. He's already taking credit for you noticing that the scene was tampered with."

Samantha chuckled at this remark. "To be honest with you, Dad." Sam paused with due consideration to make him think she was going to tell him otherwise. "Your spiel about your pajama pants riding up was exactly the reason why I noticed something wasn't right about Jenni supposedly falling."

"I knew it! You guys think all I do is bitch about things, but if I wouldn't have bitched about my pajama pants, the case could have been closed as an accident."

"Oh, Lord, this does not give you a free license to complain more," Samantha told her dad.

"I don't think he could possibly complain more than he does," Brenda retorted.

Samantha started from the beginning with the dynamics of the different personalities in the house. She was almost at the end of her saga when Dan interrupted her. "Hold that thought. I'm getting hungry, and it's still early enough to beat the dinner crowd. Let's head up to the square and see if we can get a table at Hemmingway's outside, and you can finish the story then."

Dan held off getting a drink once they got seated but instead ordered calamari to get them started. "Okay, finish the story. I'm all ears."

When Samantha finished her outline of what had gone down that night, her parents were in awe of the accumulations of events.

"You're lucky he didn't get so upset with you that he attacked you and hurt you."

"Mom, Detective Johnson was right next to me and he was armed. I wasn't worried about that—I was worried that he wouldn't crack." Samantha's eyes wandered to the table being sat next to them. Two handsome men dressed in khakis and short-sleeved button-ups sat down. Her mother's eyes followed hers and smiled.

The waitress came back to the table, and Dan ordered his Manhattan. The two gentlemen overheard and asked Dan what exactly was in a Manhattan. They stated that they were looking for something to drink with a little potency because they were stuck working on a tough case on a Saturday. Their law office was right by the square.

There were a ton of law offices dispersed throughout the streets around the square, so Samantha wasn't surprised to hear they were lawyers. This made her even more interested in the man who wasn't wearing a wedding band. *There's no better combination than a man that is good-looking* and *smart*, she thought to herself.

Instead of turning around after Dan told him what was in a Manhattan, the attractive single man commented on Sam and her parents' tans. Samantha told him her parents just got back from vacation and she was in Destin a couple weeks ago. Like most people who lived in Atlanta, he knew Destin and even owned a condo down there. She told him she had grown up there, and he recapped the places he'd been while staying there. Dan and Brenda tried to keep the conversation going between Sam and Trey, the lawyer, because they saw potential that Sam and he might be interested in each other. Dan and Trey were talking about boating when Sam excused herself to use the restroom.

On the way back from the bathroom, she came out the front of the restaurant to head to the alley where their table was seated outside. She was grinning to herself, thinking how cute Trey was and hoped there was some possibility there. She was not really paying attention to where she was walking and almost ran into someone. She looked up to apologize, and standing in front of her was Brad. Her heart seemed to stop in an instant, and she realized she had stopped breathing and had to exhale slowly. She stood frozen in place with her eyes in a wide stare of shock.

The look on his face was sheepish and uncomfortable. He knew it was not considerate of him for not responding to her texts, and you could easily tell he felt guilty for it. They both exchanged astonished greetings. Then Brad's face slowly changed as he stood staring into Sam's eyes, and everything softened about his countenance. A smile slowly formed while his gray-blue eyes crinkled. He looked at her with intense love in his eyes.

All the saliva in Sam's mouth seemed to have dried up, and it was hard for her to speak. There was a battle going on between her heart and her head. A part of her wanted to reach out and touch him and embrace the person she loved. The reasoning side of her kept her distance because she was angry and confused by everything. It made her feel dizzy. She still loved this man with every fiber in her body, but her brain was telling her that he had hurt her and he obviously didn't feel the same. She knew he wouldn't ask or say anything that could be potentially emotional because he didn't know how to deal with most touchy situations in his life. She was actually surprised he didn't immediately run in the opposite direction to avoid any type of confrontation.

Samantha finally uttered, "How are you? Wow, it's been so long. I can't believe we ran into each other. How's everyone?"

"Everything is good. How are you?"

Even though his response was typical, it still hurt her to hear him say everything was good when she'd be lying if she said she'd been well since he's been gone. She knew he would prefer to not address anything referencing their breakup, but that didn't stop Samantha from asking the probing question.

"I've been okay. It's been really hard, you know? Especially since I don't understand how it went from us being best friends and saying you still loved me to you not being able to answer my texts."

His face looked pain-stricken when she asked her question. "I just thought it was the right thing to do for both of us. I really don't want to discuss this."

"Sorry, Brad, it's something I want to know. I'm not going to avoid the purple elephant. I'm not afraid to talk about things. It's what I do for a living."

"I've told you before, Sam—it's too hard on both of us to talk."

Her mouth felt like cotton. "Too hard for both of us or you? It hurts a lot more when someone you love ignores you and doesn't explain the inconsistencies."

This was when she realized it had always been all about what Brad wanted. She spent their relationship doing what he was comfortable doing, and she was okay with that because she loved him.

But when did he ever put her needs and wants first? What sacrifices did he ever make for her? If Brad didn't like something in his life, he'd just avoid it and sweep it under the rug. All this time, she believed he loved her more than anyone. She thought their love was mutual, and she trusted him when he told her he had never been more in love and wanted to always be with her. It was so hard to get over him because she still couldn't believe he was not the person she had fallen madly in love with.

The truth was he left her when all she asked for was a deeper commitment. He was too afraid to truly give one hundred percent to anyone in his life for fear of being abandoned again.

Samantha was so preoccupied by the thoughts swimming in her head that she didn't notice that Trey had walked up to them. "I hate to interrupt, but I'm about to take your dad's advice and get a Manhattan, and I was wondering, can I order you a drink also?"

Samantha was thrilled by this gesture. *It couldn't have been better timing if I planned it myself,* she thought to herself. "You know what, Trey, order me one too."

"Sounds good. I'm holding you and your dad responsible for this drink selection."

"That's fine. After a couple of them, you won't remember who to blame." Sam flirted back.

He laughed and said, "Perfect," and walked back to his table.

As he walked away, Brad looked dejected. "I had my first Manhattan with your dad. You never drank them with us."

Sam nodded and stared into his eyes. She was sad that for some reason he couldn't give her everything she wanted. She still loved him but realized she deserved someone who didn't just want to be with her but someone who didn't want to be without her. This past year, she had been in so much pain from losing the love of her life. At times, she truly didn't want to continue to live if living was without him. Now, standing in front of her, not once did he say he missed her or he still loved her. He didn't even apologize for his unresponsiveness that plagued her emotionally. She always hoped if they ever saw each other again that he'd want her back. He didn't. He didn't love her the way she thought or they'd be together. It finally dawned on her, no matter what one has experienced in life, they usually choose to do what is best for them. He obviously didn't think she was it.

"Well, things change. Don't they, Brad?"

She turned away from him and headed back to the table. She didn't dare turn around in fear of seeing who he might be meeting or running back to him and embracing him, hoping things would change and he would be the man she loved.

She held her head high and slowly walked out of his life.

She was looking forward to sharing that drink with Trey.

ABOUT THE AUTHOR

J ENNIFER GAUL RESIDES IN Atlanta, Georgia, but grew up in Fort Walton Beach, where the book takes place. She holds a degree in social work and a master's in psychology.

CPSIA information can be obtained
at www.ICGtesting.com
Printed in the USA
FSOW01n0325280917
39079FS